The Hyacinth CHRONICLES

Other books by Patty Froese Ntihemuka

The Woman at the Well

Mary: Call Me Blessed

Martha and Mary

The Hyacinth Chronicles

CHRONICLES

Hyacinth Doesn't Go to Jail *and* Hyacinth Doesn't Miss Christmas

PATTY FROESE NTIHEMUKA

Pacific Press® Publishing Association
Nampa, Idaho
Oshawa, Ontario, Canada
www.pacificpress.com

Cover design by Gerald Lee Monks
Cover design resources from Kim Justinen
Inside design resources from Kim Justinen and iStockphoto.com
Inside design by Aaron Troia

The author assumes full responsibility for the accuracy of all facts and quotations as cited in this book.

You can obtain additional copies of this book by calling toll-free 1-800-765-6955 or by visiting www.adventistbookcenter.com.

Library of Congress Cataloging-in-Publication Data:

Ntihemuka, Patty Froese, 1978-
  Hyacinth doesn't go to jail ; and, Hyacinth doesn't miss Christmas /
Patty Froese Ntihemuka.
     p. cm. — (The Hyacinth chronicles)
  Summary: Lively and talkative Hyacinth, age six-and-three-quarters, loves her teacher and makes a new friend, but also endures encounters with the fourth-grade bully and the teasing of her older brother, Nolan, in these two stories of life in second grade.
  ISBN 13: 978-0-8163-2372-2 (pbk.)
  ISBN 10: 0-8163-2372-0 (pbk.)
  [1. Schools. 2. Brothers and sisters. 3. Family life. 4. Christian life. 5. Humorous stories.] I. Ntihemuka, Patty Froese, 1978- Hyacinth doesn't miss Christmas.
II. Title. III. Title: Hyacinth does not go to jail. IV. Title: Hyacinth doesn't miss Christmas.
  PZ7.N9626Hy 2009
  —dc22
                                                                    2009034115

09 10 11 12 13 • 5 4 3 2 1

Contents

Hyacinth Doesn't Go to Jail

Hyacinth Doesn't Miss Christmas

Book 1

Hyacinth Doesn't Go to Jail

Chapter 1

Hyacinth Gail Pipsner was six and three-quarters years old, and as of this very morning, she was officially in grade two. School was not new to her, having done grade one the previous year, and she was quite sure she knew how things worked.

Hyacinth had a brother in grade three named Nolan Bartholomew Pipsner, but if you were to call him by his full name, you had better be his mother or start running! Hyacinth's father was the pastor of the local church, and her mother worked part time in an office downtown. They did not have pets, but

Hyacinth was always hoping for a large dog. You never know when your parents might change their minds!

This particular morning, Hyacinth and her brother, Nolan, were getting ready for the first day of school.

"You'd better not miss anything," her brother said. "Grade two is harder than grade one."

"*You* did it!" she said.

"Yes, but I'm smarter than you," Nolan said.

"No, you aren't," she said. "You're just older."

"Well, you are younger, so grade two will be harder for you," he said.

Hyacinth thought about this for a minute or two. It didn't quite seem right, but she couldn't figure out how.

"I have my new backpack!" she announced. "And I have all my erasers and pencils and paper and crayons—"

"Do you have a calculator?" her brother asked.

"No," Hyacinth said, looking down into her shiny and plastic-y backpack, which was carefully packed full of the new school supplies.

"Well, you'd better have one, or you'll fall behind in math," Nolan said.

"*You* don't have one!" she said.

"Says who?" he asked.

"Says me!" she said. "I saw what Mom bought you too. And you don't have one!"

"I do," he said. "I didn't need a new one. I have mine from last year."

"Mom!" Hyacinth hollered. *"Mom!"*

"Oh, stop, Hya-Bya," Nolan said.

"Don't call me that!" she said.

"Call you what?"

"That!"

"Hya-Bya?"

"Mooooooooom!"

Mrs. Pipsner came out of the bathroom. Her hair was half combed. She held a brush in one hand. She looked down at them and shook her head.

"Nolan Bartholomew, stop teasing your sister," she said. "And Hyacinth Gail, stop that hollering! If you two act like that in school, they'll call me to come get you, and then you'll see what's what!"

"Do I need a calculator?" Hyacinth asked breathlessly. "Nolan said I do!"

"I don't think so," Mrs. Pipsner said. "I didn't see it on your list."

She disappeared into the bathroom, and the water started to run.

"What if I do?" Hyacinth asked Nolan seriously. "Then I won't have one, and all the other kids will!"

"Well," Nolan said. "Kids who don't have all their

11

supplies can get behind. It might even land you in jail."

Before Hyacinth could ask Nolan what on earth he meant and start to worry about jail, too, she saw her father poke his head out of the kitchen. "Who has eaten breakfast?" Pastor Pipsner called.

"I'm not hungry!" Hyacinth said. "And I think I need a calculator!"

"Not hungry?" her father said. "How can you not be hungry on the first day of school?"

"Daddy," Hyacinth said. "I think I need a calculator!"

"You don't need a calculator," her father said. "You need breakfast."

Pastor Pipsner stood with a pot of porridge in one hand and a spoon in the other. He gestured towards the table with the spoon and a blob of porridge plopped from it and landed on the floor. Hyacinth followed the direction of the pointing spoon and slid into her chair at the table.

"I'm nervous," she announced.

"Are you?" her father asked.

"Yes," Hyacinth said. "Too nervous to eat."

"You shouldn't be," Nolan said. "You always say that you aren't new to school. You're in grade two!"

"And you will have the same teacher," her father reminded her. "Try to eat something. Just put it in your mouth and chew and see what happens."

"We didn't say grace!" Nolan said.

"Say grace, Nolan," Pastor Pipsner said.

"Dear God," Nolan said, bowing his head. "Thank You for the porridge. And the milk. And the sugar. Amen."

"You didn't say thank You for the toast!" Hyacinth said.

"And the toast and the first day of school," Pastor Pipsner said. "Now eat!"

Twenty-five minutes later, Hyacinth and Nolan stood outside their house, their backpacks on their backs. The big yellow bus lumbered up and slowed down to a stop. Hyacinth turned around and looked at the window where her parents were standing. Her father's arm draped around her mother's shoulders. They waved and smiled and nodded to her. There was a flash in the window, and Hyacinth was pretty sure her mother had taken a picture.

"I feel lonely," Hyacinth said, her voice quivering.

"Don't feel lonely," Nolan said. "I don't."

Hyacinth stepped into the bus behind her brother. The air was warm and smelled like orange peels and brown bread sandwiches. The front of the bus had the little grade ones, and the back of the bus had the high school kids. Hyacinth stood in terror, looking at all the filled seats. Nolan found an empty one and sat down in it.

Hyacinth looked at the little kids. They were staring up at her with wide eyes. She looked at the big kids who seemed old enough to drive and vote, and she thought that she just might cry!

"Cinthy," Nolan called, and he slid over in his seat.

Hyacinth thought that she had the best brother in the whole world just then, and she instantly forgave him for all his teasing.

"Look, Mom is taking a picture of the bus," Nolan said, and Hyacinth looked out the bus window to see her mother standing in front of the house, her camera held up to her face. There was another flash.

"I'm sure you can see me in that picture!" Hyacinth said. "And she'll put it in the scrapbook!"

The bus lurched forward and started the long ride to Highview Christian Academy.

"Hey, Nolan," Hyacinth said.

"What?"

"Do I really need a calculator?"

Chapter 2

Highview Christian Academy was made of two big buildings. One was the high school for the older kids, and one was the elementary school for the younger kids. Hyacinth was in grade two, so she was in Mrs. Raju's class again. Mrs. Raju taught both grade one and grade two together in the same room. The grade one kids sat closer to the window, and the grade two kids sat closer to the door.

"Welcome back, Hyacinth!" Mrs. Raju said, smiling her big, white-toothed smile at Hyacinth. Mrs. Raju was plump, with shining black hair and eyes that crinkled at the corners.

"Hi, Mrs. Raju!" Hyacinth said, feeling a little bit shy.

Hyacinth and her mother had visited the classroom a few days earlier, and Mrs. Raju had shown Hyacinth where her cubby would be and where her desk would sit so she knew just where to put her outdoor shoes and her lunch box. She knew just where to hang her backpack and her jacket.

Mrs. Raju stood in front of the door to the classroom, holding it open.

"Come inside, kids!" she called.

The grade ones looked kind of scared, and most of them had their moms or dads with them. One boy was crying, and his mom was pushing him towards Mrs. Raju. One girl turned around and ran away. Her dad was too slow to snag her on her way by, and he had to run after her down the hallway.

Hyacinth went with the other kids into the classroom and found her desk. She opened her backpack and began to carefully put her things inside. She put her notebooks and her pencils in the desk, her eraser and her glue stick, and her crayons and her ruler. She nodded to herself. It was just right!

"Welcome to a brand-new school year!" Mrs. Raju said. "Please sit in your seats. We are going to say a prayer before we begin."

So Hyacinth bowed her head and only peeked a little bit

while Mrs. Raju prayed. She was peeking because she liked to watch Mrs. Raju's white teeth when she talked. When Mrs. Raju said "Amen," Hyacinth looked up to see another girl looking at her very seriously.

"You didn't close your eyes," the girl said. She had black hair with very small curls. It was arranged in little braids all over her head.

"Did you?" Hyacinth whispered.

"No, I was watching you," she said. "I'm Ruby."

"I'm Hyacinth."

"Hya-what?"

"Hyacinth. It's a flower."

"Oh, mine is a jewel. Can I call you Cinthy?"

"OK," said Hyacinth. "Are you *new*?"

"I see that you have met Ruby, Hyacinth," Mrs. Raju said. "Please listen to our worship story now and get acquainted later."

Hyacinth listened to the story about a boy who was new in school and how the other kids made him feel at home. She liked the story and hoped she could help Ruby feel at home like the kids in the story did for the new boy.

After another prayer, Mrs. Raju said to Hyacinth, "Would you and Ruby like to be buddies this year?"

"What do buddies do?" Ruby asked.

"We line up together and tell the teacher if one of us is

missing," said Hyacinth. "And we go to the bathroom together so we don't get lost down the big kids' hall."

"What's the big kids' hall?"

"It's where the big grade fives and sixes are," Hyacinth said. "My brother said that there was once a girl who wandered down that hall, and no one could find her till lunchtime!"

Mrs. Raju rang a little bell over her head.

"Grade ones!" she called. "Over to the carpet for story time! Grade twos, I want you to write your names on the pieces of cardboard on your desks. Do it carefully and make it beautiful, because we are going to have them on the front of your desks for the rest of the year."

Hyacinth felt very proud to be a grade two. She felt proud that she was entrusted to write her own name, not just decorate around the name the teacher had written. She felt proud that she could answer when the teacher said, "Grade twos!"

So Hyacinth took one of the fat markers that smelled like blue candy and stared thoughtfully at the cardboard. This was a decision that would last all year long. Should she write her whole name, *Hyacinth Gail Pipsner,* which she could now spell very well, or should she just write *Hyacinth*? With her very best printing and her tongue stuck out the side of her mouth, she began to write her name, her marker squeaking across the card.

H-y-a-c-i-n-t-h.

But the card was running out of space, so as she wrote, the letters started to get smaller and smaller.

G-a-i-l.

P-i-p.

The *Pip* was very small, and the last *p* was squeezed right at the end of the card. There was no more space! She looked at the other kids' cards, and they all seemed to be the same size. Her name was just too long! There was a *sner* that was missing and no space to put it in!

Hyacinth raised her hand and looked around for Mrs. Raju, but Mrs. Raju was busy with the grade ones on the carpet.

"Oh dear," she said under her breath, staring at the card. Then an idea came to her. She'd just turn it over! But when she did, she saw the marker had soaked through to the other side.

"Oh dear," she murmured again.

"Hyacinth Gail Pip!" a boy said and laughed, and she gave him a very stern look.

"That is *not* my name," she said. "It is only part of it."

"Miss Pip!" he said. "Miss Pip!"

"Stop it!" Hyacinth said.

"Miss Pip!"

"What is happening over there, grade twos?" Mrs. Raju called, standing up from the story circle.

Hyacinth could feel her face go all warm with anger and embarrassment. She would *not* repeat that foul name. She would *not*!

"Nothing," said the boy.

"Nothing," said Hyacinth.

Mrs. Raju gave them a stern look and shook her head so that her shiny black hair swung around her face like a curtain. Then she sat back down on the story rug with the grade ones.

"You could just draw a picture over the *Pip* part," said Ruby. "Then you'd be Hyacinth Gail."

"Huh," said Hyacinth. With a few more squeaks of the marker, she sat back in satisfaction.

"What is it?" asked Ruby.

"I don't know," said Hyacinth. "I think it's a dog."

"Are you sure?" asked Ruby.

"Or a bat," said Hyacinth.

"It could be a bat," Ruby agreed with a nod. "But what is pretty about a bat?"

"It can sense things in the dark when it can't see," Hyacinth announced proudly. "I'm pretty sure I can do that too!"

As she sat down to color in the flowers and balloons around her name and the bat, Hyacinth decided she needed to say a prayer.

"Dear God," she prayed very quietly. "I don't like that boy. But I like Ruby, so thank You for my new friend! And help me to stop feeling so mad at that boy. Or maybe You could ruin his card too! But if You think that's no fair, then maybe You could help me to stop feeling so mad at that boy. Amen."

Hyacinth colored one more flower and carefully added some leaves.

"Oh," she prayed. "I almost forgot. I'm sorry to have watched the teacher's teeth during prayer! I'll try not to do that."

And Hyacinth did feel better.

Chapter 3

Hyacinth was a girl who liked to talk. There were a great many things that needed to be said. Sometimes, something odd needed to be pointed out. Sometimes, something funny needed to be laughed at. Sometimes, the silence was just begging to be filled! That was never a problem because Hyacinth had a lot of thoughts running through her mind, and several of them were worth saying out loud at once.

Hyacinth's mother called her "talkative," and her father called her his "little chatterbox." Nolan called her "noisy," but then brothers do tend to tease their sisters whenever they can. Hyacinth didn't think that she talked a lot. She never noticed!

"Hyacinth!"

Hyacinth looked up at Mrs. Raju. She stood with her arms crossed over her chest, and her lips pressed together in a thin line.

"Please do your work *quietly,*" Mrs. Raju said, and put one finger up against her lips.

"Yes, Mrs. Raju," Hyacinth said. She felt her face go pink. She hated getting in trouble with the teacher!

Hyacinth was working on her math. There was a row of numbers that needed to be added together.

$$4 + 2 + 1 + 3 = \underline{\hspace{2cm}}.$$

Hyacinth liked math. Math wasn't so hard! First, you took the 4, and then you added the 2. That made 6. Then, you added the 1. That made 7. Then, you added the 3—that made 10! The answer was 10!

She wrote 10 in the space, pressing so hard with her pencil that she nearly broke the tip. Again. She hated working with a blunt pencil, and there was nothing worse than doing math with a pencil with a broken tip! When that happened, Hyacinth knew she could go to Mrs. Raju's desk and carefully sharpen her pencil to a beautiful point!

"Ruby!" Hyacinth whispered.

"What?" said Ruby.

"Did you get ten for number four?"

"I got eight."

"Uh-oh. I got ten."

"Who is right?"

"Let's do it again."

So Hyacinth added the numbers again. She took the 4 and added the 2. That made 6. Then she added the 1. That made 7. Then she added the 3. *10!*

"I still got ten," Hyacinth whispered.

"I still got eight," Ruby replied.

"How'd you get eight?" Hyacinth asked. "I don't get it!"

"Hyacinth, please!" Mrs. Raju said, her calm, reassuring voice started to sound a little frustrated. "You need to work by yourself. Just do your work, and if you have a question, raise your hand and I will come to you."

Hyacinth clamped her mouth shut and sighed. Math wasn't hard, but being quiet during math sure was! She looked at the other kids. They were hunched over their papers. Carl was erasing and erasing—erasing so hard that Hyacinth wondered if he wouldn't rub a hole in his paper! Lisa was writing ever so neatly, her ankles crossed under her desk, and her white socks gleaming very, very white over the top of her smooth, black indoor shoes. Lisa always looked this clean. It seemed impossible to Hyacinth, and she always had the urge to rub some dirt onto those gleaming white socks!

"Lisa's socks are so white!" Hyacinth whispered.

"Whose socks?" Ruby asked.

"Lisa's—see? Over there!"

Ruby turned to look, and Hyacinth covered her mouth to giggle. She turned back to her page to work on the next math problem. Just then she saw the dark shadow of someone standing over her desk. She looked up, up, up until she saw crossed arms—and up a little more until she saw the very unhappy face of Mrs. Raju.

"*Hyacinth.*"

Hyacinth looked up in silence. She considered saying, "Mrs. Raju," but changed her mind.

"What is so important that you need to talk?"

"Nothing," Hyacinth said.

"Are you sure you don't want to share with the class? It

seemed very funny," Mrs. Raju said.

"I don't think everyone would find it funny," Hyacinth said truthfully.

Hyacinth noticed that the whole class was now looking at her instead of their math papers. The grade ones looked somewhat terrified. The grade twos looked amused.

"Hyacinth, I think we need to change where you sit," Mrs. Raju said. "Ruby needs to get her math done, and so do you."

Hyacinth looked up in horror! Mrs. Raju was going to move Hyacinth's desk!

"Stand up, please," Mrs. Raju said.

Hyacinth mutely stood up. Mrs. Raju dragged Hyacinth's desk across the floor, the little rubber feet squeaking shamefully across the squares of gray linoleum. She watched, horrified, as Mrs. Raju dragged her desk all the way around the room. She stopped, right in front of her big teacher desk, with the pencil sharpener screwed to the top and the pile of penmanship books waiting to be corrected. Hyacinth took a deep breath and walked mournfully after her desk. She refused to look at the other children, who she *knew* were staring.

Hyacinth Gail Pipsner had just been punished! She let out a sigh and sank into her seat, facing the teacher's desk. She looked down at her paper. She would *not* look up at

Mrs. Raju! She would *not*! She did not want to see the look on her teacher's face. Hyacinth was already ashamed enough!

"Now, class," Mrs. Raju said. "Let us start with number four. Who has the answer and can tell us how they got it?"

Hyacinth looked down at her paper. She had the answer to number four. She'd checked it twice, and she was sure she had it!

"Ruby?" Mrs. Raju asked.

"Eight?" Ruby didn't sound very sure.

"No, not eight," Mrs. Raju said. "But nice try. Anyone else?"

There was some rustling, but Hyacinth did not turn around to look at the class. She sat with her back straight and her head down, staring at her paper.

"Hyacinth?" Mrs. Raju said.

Hyacinth shook her head. No, she would not answer. She was being punished for being too noisy, and she was not going to talk now!

"Twelve?" Carl offered.

"No, but good try, Carl," Mrs. Raju said. She looked at the little watch on her wrist.

"We have five minutes until the buses arrive, kids!" she announced. "We have no more time for math today. We will start with number four tomorrow. Thank you for a good day, and I will see you tomorrow!"

Hyacinth stood up and slowly put her papers back in her desk. This was not a good day. It was not a good day at all! It was a miserable day, and Hyacinth thought she might like to cry.

"Goodbye, Hyacinth," Mrs. Raju said kindly. "I will move your desk back to its spot for tomorrow morning. I'm sure tomorrow you will be much quieter."

Hyacinth gave a silent little wave and plodded towards her cubby where her outdoor shoes, backpack, and jacket were waiting for her. She would *not* speak. If quiet was what they wanted, quiet was what they'd get. She felt a lump rising in her throat, and her eyes brimmed with tears.

Hyacinth put on her outdoor shoes, pushed her arms into her jacket, and hoisted her backpack onto her back. Then she turned and looked into the classroom where Mrs. Raju was erasing the chalkboard.

"The answer is *ten*!" Hyacinth declared, her voice echoing through the classroom. And with that, she dashed out to her bus.

Chapter 4

While Pastor Pipsner washed the dishes after supper that night, Hyacinth and Nolan stood side by side in front of the sink, holding their tea (dish) towels. It was their job to dry. Hyacinth watched very closely as Nolan took a spoon from the sink and began to dry it.

"You took a spoon!" Hyacinth said.

"So?" said Nolan.

"So, it isn't fair!" Hyacinth said. "I dried a bowl!"

"So?" said Nolan. "A bowl might be bigger, but a spoon has more curves and edges!"

"My towel is wetter!" Hyacinth said.

"That's because you don't let the water drip off things before you dry them," said Nolan.

Hyacinth looked into the sink. There were no more spoons, just plates. So she took one and started to dry it. Her towel was soaked, though, and it just wiped the water around on the plate. She watched as Nolan put his hand into the sink. He'd have to take a plate now! But just as Nolan put his hand into the sink, her father dropped something else into the sink, and Nolan emerged with another spoon! He gave her a triumphant look.

"No fair!" Hyacinth said, and her lip started to quiver.

"Don't be a baby," said Nolan.

"I'm not!" Hyacinth said. "But I had a really bad day."

"What happened?" her father asked.

"I got in trouble," Hyacinth said. "And I didn't mean to! I made a new friend, and her name is Ruby. I like her a lot. She has hair that has these little tiny curls in it, and she wears it in little braids all over her head. It's pretty! And she's new!"

"You got in trouble for making a friend?" her father asked in confusion.

"No, for talking to her during math," Hyacinth said, sighing sadly. "I didn't mean to!"

"What happened?" her brother asked her, his eyes shining with interest.

"Mrs. Raju—" Hyacinth stopped, her cheeks feeling hot with embarrassment.

"What?" asked Nolan.

"Come on," her father said. "What did Mrs. Raju do?"

"She moved my desk," Hyacinth sighed. "It was terrible!"

"Oh, is that all?" Nolan asked.

"What do you mean?" Hyacinth exclaimed, "I've never had my desk moved before! And it was in front of everyone!"

"You could have been sent to the principal's office," Nolan said, giving Hyacinth a wise look.

"What happens there?" she breathed.

"Punishment!" Nolan replied. "With a capital *P*!"

"Oh!" Hyacinth said, her eyes wide.

"Don't you worry about it," her father said, wringing out the dishcloth and hanging it over the tap. "The principal's office is reserved for the bad kids. You couldn't be bad enough to be sent there!"

He gave her shoulder a reassuring squeeze.

"You kids finish drying," Pastor Pipsner said. "I'm going to go find your mother."

Hyacinth watched him go and turned her attention back to the sink and the last of the dishes.

"Hey!" Hyacinth exclaimed. "Where did you find another spoon?"

Nolan shrugged.

"I'd hate to have to visit you in jail," he said after a moment of silence.

"Why in jail?" asked Hyacinth.

"Well, the government lets the school system deal with you first," he said. "And if they are unsuccessful, well—"

"Then you go to jail?" Hyacinth asked, aghast.

"Well, someone has to straighten you out!" Nolan said.

After the dishes were done and after the Pipsner family had worship together, Hyacinth still didn't feel very happy. It had been an awful day, and she just couldn't feel better again! She was also more than a little worried that jail might be in her future.

Hyacinth's Grammy lived far away in Canada. She worked in a tall building that was made of shiny glass. She had an office with a big wooden desk and a phone that looked like it did much more than the Pipsner phone at home. Hyacinth was allowed to call her grammy any time she wanted, because, as Hyacinth's mother always said, their family had a "good long distance plan."

"You pay a bit, but it's worth it, not having to count the minutes!" was how her mother put it.

So Hyacinth decided it was time to call her grammy. Hyacinth looked up at the numbers written on the page that was tacked up on the side of the cupboard, and she carefully dialed the number printed there. It rang once. It rang twice. It rang three times. Just when Hyacinth was about to give up hope, her grammy's voice came on the other end.

"Hello?" Grammy said.

"Grammy, it's me, Hyacinth!" Hyacinth said.

"Hello, my girl!" Grammy said, her voice warm and happy. "I just got back from a long day at work. Just got in now! What perfect timing you have!"

"Oh, I'm glad!" Hyacinth sighed.

"How are you, dear?" her grammy asked.

"Not so good." Hyacinth sighed.

"Why not?"

"I had a bad day at school," Hyacinth replied. "I got in trouble!"

And the story spilled out of her like milk from a cup! After she'd told all of it, she felt a little bit better.

"That's terrible!" Grammy said. "What a day!"

"I know," Hyacinth sighed. "Grade two is turning out to be harder than I thought!"

"Would you like to hear a story?" Grammy asked.

"OK," said Hyacinth.

"Well," said Grammy. "Today at work, when I went

downstairs for my lunch break, I saw the saddest little cat you ever could see."

"And?" said Hyacinth.

"Poor little thing. It looked just miserable! It kept trying to come into the building where it was warm. It looked so hungry!"

"What did you do?" Hyacinth asked.

"Well, I picked that little cat up, and I brought her upstairs," Grammy said. "I took her all the way up to the twenty-seventh floor where my office is, and I took her into our break room where there is a refrigerator."

"And?" said Hyacinth.

"I took some cream that we use for hot drinks, and I poured it into a bowl and let that cat have all the cream she wanted," Grammy said.

"She must have liked that!" Hyacinth said.

"Oh, she did," Grammy agreed. "In fact, I thought I would take that little cat home with me and take care of her."

"Did you?" Hyacinth asked.

"I got permission to leave work early. I took the elevator down, and I took that cat outside to walk to my car," Grammy said. "And as soon as we got outside, she jumped out of my arms and ran away!"

"Oh no!" Hyacinth said.

"No, dear, it's all right," Grammy said. "That little cat didn't need to come home with me. She was just sad and lonely and needed some cream and a cuddle."

"Really?" said Hyacinth.

"And when she got back outside, she was ready to go face the world again!" Grammy said.

"You think I need cream and a cuddle?" Hyacinth asked.

"I think so, dear," said Grammy.

"Oh, Grammy?" Hyacinth said.

"Yes, dear?"

"Nolan only dries spoons!" Hyacinth said. "Just so you know!"

Grammy chuckled, said she loved Hyacinth, and Hyacinth hung up the phone. Then she went to the kitchen, poured herself a nice cup of milk, and wandered downstairs to the family room where her mother was sitting, reading her Bible in the big swivel rocking chair.

"Hi, sweetie!" her mother said.

"Hi," said Hyacinth, and she crawled up into the big swivel rocking chair and wriggled in next to her mother. She leaned her head against her mother's chest and listened to the *lub-dub* sound of her heart.

"I love you, Hyacinth," her mother said, giving her a loud kiss on her forehead.

"Me, too, Mommy," Hyacinth said.

And Grammy was right. Everything looked much better from here.

Chapter 5

The next day, Hyacinth's desk was back to its usual place. Right before school started, Ruby gave her a beautiful unicorn eraser as a token that they would be friends forever. "Thank you so much," she told Ruby just as Mrs. Raju called the room to order. She quickly put the eraser into her pocket for safekeeping.

After worship that morning, they looked at leaves and learned what the veins were for. The teacher wrote a shockingly long word on the chalkboard: *photosynthesis.* Hyacinth had never seen a longer word. But before she knew it, it was recess time.

"Come on!" said Ruby. "Let's go play on the jungle gym!"

"The boys got it first," Hyacinth said.

"Then the swings!" said Ruby, and she ran off towards the swings to make sure she got one. Hyacinth, however, realized at that moment that she desperately needed to use the bathroom.

"I'll be back!" she called after Ruby. "Save me a swing!"

She turned back toward the school. The hallway was very dark compared to the bright sunlight outside. She could hear the muffled voices of other classes that weren't in recess. She looked down the long, dim hallway. Where was the bathroom again?

She walked past the grade three and four room. She could see the older kids leaning over their desks through the little window in the door. She would have tried to see Nolan, but she didn't want to get into trouble.

At the end of the hallway, she realized that she hadn't seen the bathroom. That was odd. Where was it again? She stood facing another hallway, and she was about to venture down it when she stopped short. The big kids' hallway! This was the one she'd been warned about!

She looked back the way she had come. She looked down the big kids' hallway. Well, she needed a bathroom, so it seemed there was no choice! Hyacinth put her chin up and bravely went on.

"What are you doing down here?" a voice demanded.

Hyacinth looked up into the face of a boy. He was the biggest boy she'd ever seen! He was tall and big. His hair wasn't combed, and he looked as if he had slept in his clothes. He squinted his eyes down to little slits and screwed up his mouth.

"Huh, kid?" he said. "You are far from the babies' room!"

"I'm not a baby!" Hyacinth declared. "I'm in grade two!"

"Grade two?" The boy laughed. "Grade two!"

Hyacinth stared up at the great big boy. He was huge! He was horrible! He looked mean.

"Where is your hall pass?" he said.

"I don't have one!" she replied.

"Then you're in trouble!" he said. "You'll have to pay me to keep quiet."

"I don't have any money," Hyacinth said.

"What's that?" he said, pointing to the bulge in Hyacinth's pocket.

"My unicorn eraser," she replied, pulling it out of her pocket. The eraser was so beautiful that she wouldn't ever erase with it because it might get ruined.

"Give it to me," the boy said.

"What?" Hyacinth's voice shook.

"Give . . . it . . . to . . . me," the big boy said, leaning his face close to Hyacinth. His breath smelled like mustard sandwiches, and his hair looked greasy close up. Hyacinth looked at him in horror.

"Now!" he snapped.

With a yelp of terror, Hyacinth threw her precious unicorn eraser in his general direction before dashing back down the hallway.

She ran and ran. She didn't care where she went, as long as it was away from that horrible, mustard-smelling boy! Suddenly, she saw the little sign for the girls' bathroom. It looked like a girl in a skirt, and she skidded to a stop. Glancing back and seeing no one, she rushed inside, pushed the door shut, and leaned against it, breathing hard.

That boy must have been the grade four bully. He is even more horrible than Nolan's stories about him! She shuddered at the memory. Tears welled up in her eyes as she thought about her unicorn eraser. Ruby had given it to her, and she loved it! It was their token of forever friendship, and now that horrible, big boy had it in his sweaty, smelly hand!

It was then that Hyacinth realized that she didn't recognize this bathroom. It wasn't the one she normally used. The walls were a different color, and the stalls were on the wrong side. It was like a bad dream. Where was she?

While she tried to figure that out, Hyacinth used the bathroom quickly. She decided she had two choices. She could stay here in this strange bathroom, or she could go back out *there* and see if she could find the grade one and two classroom. She had been gone an awfully long time, she was sure. Recess was probably over by now, and Ruby would be wondering why she hadn't gone to the swings.

"Well, I can't stay in here forever," Hyacinth reasoned with herself. "Then I'd miss my bus home too!"

The thought of being alone in this bathroom all night long was not a good one. So she plucked up her courage and poked her head out the bathroom door. She didn't see anyone. She could hear the sound of another class being told, "Walk, children. No running!" on their way out to recess.

"Dear God," Hyacinth prayed. "Help me to find my room, and help the bully to not find me!"

And with that, she ventured out into the hallway.

"I'll go that way," she said to herself. "And if I can't find my room, I'll turn around and go the other way!"

So Hyacinth trotted off down the hallway, looking this

way and that. She had almost given up, but then she noticed a light at the end of the hallway. She hurried up, and when she looked around the corner, there was another shorter hallway. And what was at the end of that hallway made her break into a grin!

It was the grade one and two classroom! The one with the colorful cubbies to hold their shoes, and the little hooks to hold their coats. Hyacinth was so happy that she skipped all the way up to the door!

"Thank You, God!" she whispered, and she put her hand on the doorknob. But it didn't turn! She was locked out!

Oh no, she thought. *I'm locked out! Late kids are locked out! I'm a late kid!*

Hyacinth could hear the sound of Mrs. Raju's voice explaining something. She heard Carl ask a question, and she heard Lisa giggle about something. Then she heard the whirring sound of the electric pencil sharpener. Hyacinth lifted her hand and gave a little knock, a very soft knock.

She waited. Nothing.

She lifted her hand and knocked again, this time louder. Nothing.

Just as she was about to pound as hard as she could, the door swung open and she stared up into Mrs. Raju's surprised face.

"There you are!" she exclaimed. "I was just about to come looking for you!"

"You were?" Hyacinth squeaked.

"Of course!" Mrs. Raju said. "Where were you, Hyacinth?"

"I got lost!" Hyacinth said. "I was trying to find the bathroom, and I got all turned around." She lowered her voice and gave her teacher a significant look. "I found myself down the big kids' hallway."

"Ah," said Mrs. Raju knowingly. "Well, I'm glad you are back safely."

"Thanks," Hyacinth sighed, glad that her teacher understood what she had endured.

"What could we all do to make sure that this doesn't happen again?" Mrs. Raju asked the class.

"We could tie a string to Hyacinth's foot so she could follow it back," Carl suggested.

Mrs. Raju's eyebrows furrowed, and she shook her head.

"I was thinking more of something we could all do so that this doesn't happen to any of us," she said.

"The buddy system!" they called out.

"That's right!" Mrs. Raju said. "Everyone stay with your buddy."

As Hyacinth slid into her seat next to Ruby, she breathed a sigh of relief.

"I was worried!" Ruby whispered.

"I have something to tell you," Hyacinth whispered back. "Our friendship eraser is gone!"

Hyacinth and Ruby shared a sad look.

"What happened?" Ruby asked.

"The grade four bully!" Hyacinth said.

"The grade four bully?" Ruby asked, a look of horror on her face.

Come next recess time, Hyacinth had a story to tell. But for now, she decided it would be a good idea to be quiet. She was still figuring out grade two, after all.

Chapter 6

Recess was the highlight of every school day. There was one morning recess, one afternoon recess, and one lunchtime recess that was extra long. Recess times were organized so that only one classroom had recess at a time. The teacher would stand by the door and ring a big bell: *Clang! Clang! Clang!* And then you knew that your recess time was over and it was time to go back into school. Sometimes, while Hyacinth was doing her schoolwork in the classroom, she could hear the *clang, clang, clang* of another teacher's bell, calling another class back in from their recess. And when that happened, Hyacinth liked to stop and wonder who was being called in, and what they had done during their recess time.

One day, just before recess time, Mrs. Raju called for the children's attention.

"Today, children," said Mrs. Raju. "The grade three and four class is going to join us for recess."

"Why?" someone asked.

"Because they watched a special video and it went long, so they will have the same recess time as we will," Mrs. Raju said. "Let's all be extra polite today and share the playground."

"Grade three and four?" Hyacinth whispered excitedly. "That's my brother's class!"

"Really?" said Ruby.

"Sure is!" said Hyacinth. She was awfully proud and couldn't wait to see Nolan.

"Your brother is in grade three, right?" Carl asked.

"Yep," said Hyacinth. "I'm sure he'll want to play with me."

"Grade three and four kids never want to play with us," Carl said, not looking convinced.

"Well, Nolan is my brother, Carl," Hyacinth said, putting on her most adult expression. "He will want to play with me. He'll be very happy to see me."

Carl shrugged and Hyacinth and Ruby exchanged a look of prim disapproval. Boys could be so silly sometimes!

"I'll introduce you to my brother, Ruby," Hyacinth said. "And I'm sure he'll introduce us to his friends too!"

"You think?" asked Ruby, her eyes glowing. "Carl will have to eat his words then! Everyone will see us playing with the grade threes!"

Hyacinth smiled happily to herself. This was the best part of having an older brother! And she couldn't wait to see him!

As they ran outside, Hyacinth and Ruby looked around. The grade threes and fours were already outside playing. There were some boys, along with the bully, playing with a ball in the field. Some girls were swinging, and another group was playing a loud game of tag on the jungle gym. Over by the teeter-totters, Hyacinth spotted her brother.

"There he is!" Hyacinth said. "It's Nolan!"

And they ran off toward Nolan, where he was kicking gravel with some other boys. Nolan looked up as Hyacinth arrived, a look of surprise on his face.

"Hey, Nolan!" Hyacinth said. "We have recess with you today!"

"Oh boy," he said, looking back down to the gravel. "Well, you'd better go to the sandbox or something."

"How come?" Hyacinth asked, feeling a little hurt. "We want to play with you. This is Ruby."

"Hi," Nolan said, glancing in Ruby's direction. "You can't play with us."

"Why not?" Hyacinth demanded.

"We don't want to," Nolan said. The boys with him snickered.

"How come?" Hyacinth asked, feeling deeply wounded.

"Because you're little girls!" Nolan exclaimed. "That's why! Now leave us alone, Hyacinth!"

Hyacinth lifted her chin high, reached out for Ruby's hand, and marched away. Her lip was quivering, but she would *not* look back! If Nolan didn't want to play with her, then they'd just have to play by themselves.

"That wasn't nice," Ruby said sadly.

"No, it wasn't," Hyacinth agreed. "And I'm mad at him! You just wait and see! I won't speak to him for five weeks! And then he'll be sorry!"

"Not at all?" Ruby asked, looking impressed.

"Not even to tell him to get out of the bathroom!" Hyacinth declared with pride. "Not even to ask him to pass the food!"

Nolan didn't seem to notice he was being ignored on the bus ride home. He was talking to some other kids, and even when she gave him stern looks and pursed her lips, he didn't seem to notice. Once he passed her a tissue, though, as if he thought she was going to sneeze.

When they got off the bus, Nolan still didn't seem to notice that Hyacinth was ignoring him.

"Did you know that dinosaurs were bigger than the house?" Nolan was saying. "What a great video that was! It showed a dinosaur that stood taller than the gym!" Nolan shook his head in amazement, but Hyacinth stayed silent. She would *not* answer him!

"Some only ate plants and they were called *herbivores*," Nolan went on. "Some ate animals, and they were called *carnivores*. They even ate each other!"

Hyacinth was silent.

"You should have seen the T. rex!" Nolan said. "Jaws like this and these little tiny hands—" He made a demonstration that almost made Hyacinth laugh. She would have laughed if she were still not officially angry with Nolan.

Nolan walked on toward the house, chattering away about dinosaurs and their bones, and how paleontologists found bones all over the place. There might even be dinosaur bones in their yard for all they knew! Hyacinth found this fascinating and wanted to ask Nolan if they could dig up the yard and look for bones, but she did not. She was still angry with Nolan and couldn't speak to him.

During supper, Nolan started to notice the Hyacinth wouldn't talk to him.

"Hey, Hyacinth," Nolan said, "guess how small the smallest dinosaur is."

Hyacinth looked up at him and then back down to her plate.

"Guess!" he said.

She remained silent.

"Come on, Hya-Bya, guess!" he said.

While it was nearly *painful* to not say something back when he called her that awful name, Hyacinth still remained silent.

"How come she won't talk to me?" Nolan asked.

"Hyacinth, why won't you talk to your brother?" Mrs. Pipsner asked.

"Because he hurt my feelings!" said Hyacinth. "At recess, he wouldn't play with me and told me to go away!"

"Well, that wasn't very nice," Mr. Pipsner said.

"I didn't think she'd take it so hard," Nolan muttered. "She should know I was busy with my friends."

It was a quiet dinner. It was a quiet evening. And it was a quiet bedtime. Hyacinth lay in her bed, wiggling her toes in the cool sheets. But even wiggling her toes in cool sheets didn't make her feel happy like it usually did. She hated fighting with Nolan. Even when she was right!

After lying in bed for quite some time, she flipped back her quilt and hopped out of bed. She crept to her bedroom door and looked out into the hallway. Her brother's room was dark. She tiptoed to his door and pushed it open. Her brother lay in his bed with his back to her. But she could tell he was awake.

"Nolan?" she whispered.

He didn't answer her.

"Nolan?" she whispered again, and she sat down on the side of his bed.

"I didn't mean to hurt your feelings, you know," Nolan said after a minute.

"It's OK," said Hyacinth.

"Sorry," he said uncomfortably.

"It's OK," Hyacinth answered. "But I have to tell you, Nolan, without me around to stop you once in a while; you sure do talk a lot!"

Chapter 7

Sabbath was a busy day in the Pipsner house. Pastor Pipsner had to be at church on time, and that meant everyone else had to be ready too. So the morning was a flurry of activity. But by the end of it, Hyacinth was wearing her yellow dress with the lace around the edges. She was wearing her tights and the white shoes that went with her dress. Hyacinth was very proud of those shoes because they weren't little girl shoes with the strap over the top; they were "lady" shoes that she could slip her foot into and take her foot out of just like a grown-up lady.

"They are kind of slippery on the bottom, though," Hyacinth confessed as her mother helped her to put barrettes in her hair.

"Then you just have to walk nicely, like ladies do," her mother said.

"They almost have a heel on them, don't they?" Hyacinth asked, looking lovingly down at her shoes.

"No, honey, you aren't old enough for high heels," her mother said.

Hyacinth looked down at her shoes. Maybe they weren't high, but they were shaped like a lady's shoe, just without a high heel! And she was awfully proud of them.

When they got to church, Hyacinth practiced walking on the carpet with her "lady" shoes. She liked the way they felt, and she liked the way they looked! They only thing she didn't like was how her tights would get all baggy around her ankles. Hyacinth would tug them up, and her mother would always tap her on the shoulder and say, "Hyacinth, young ladies do not tug on their tights in front of gentlemen." Hyacinth had an image in her head of the ladies' washroom full of women

53

tugging on their nylons while they chatted about "lady" things.

After Sabbath School, Hyacinth and Nolan went to find their mother. She was sitting in the pew they always sat in, right in the middle of the church. Hyacinth sat down next to her mother and picked up the bulletin. The bulletin was the paper that said the order that everything would happen. She liked to scan down the bulletin and see her father's name there.

Opening prayer: Pastor Pipsner
Call to worship: Pastor Pipsner
Sermon: Pastor Pipsner
Closing Prayer: Pastor Pipsner

There were other people's names in there who were doing other things for the worship service, but she wasn't looking for their names. She was looking for her father's name.

"Look who is telling the children's story!" Nolan whispered, looking over her shoulder. The children's story happened before the sermon. Hyacinth always looked forward to the children's story because it was more fun than her father's sermons.

Hyacinth looked at her bulletin. Across from the words "Children's Story" was the name—

"Mrs. Raju?" Hyacinth said.

"Huh!" said Nolan. "I wonder if she'll tell a story about you being bad."

Hyacinth looked at her brother in shock. It was a possibility! Lots of people told stories that started, "There was once a little girl . . ." Those stories *always* ended with the little girl doing something horrible. Hyacinth had wondered where the storytellers got those stories. Maybe Mrs. Raju got her stories from real life!

"She wouldn't!" Hyacinth gasped.

"I don't know," Nolan shrugged. "But you'll know it if she says the girl in her story is named Hyacinth."

Hyacinth started to worry. What if Mrs. Raju told a story about Hyacinth, but changed her name? Would everyone know still? Would they guess? What would the story be about? Maybe about a girl named Theodoxria who wouldn't stop talking in math class and had to have her desk moved!

Hyacinth shuddered at the thought.

Before long, the pianist started playing the familiar music that meant it was time for the children's story. All the children knew that they were to go to the front of the church when the music played. Hyacinth glanced at Nolan on her way past him. He said he was too old for children's story, so he didn't go up front anymore. But Hyacinth still did.

Well, thought Hyacinth. *I'll just go up as ladylike as I can, and no one will guess the story is about me!*

It was as if the very thought of walking like a lady made her clumsy, because as soon as Hyacinth began walking down the aisle, her slippery shoes got away from her. When she stepped forward, one foot just kept on going and going! Like a ski on snow! Her feet flew up, and her bottom landed on the carpet right in the middle of the aisle!

There was a gasp and a ripple of laughter. Hyacinth felt some hands under her arms, pulling her back to her feet. She looked up into the face of her brother.

"Come on," he said, tugging her arm. "You're too old for the children's story anyhow."

Hyacinth tried to swallow her tears as she followed her brother back to the pew. An old lady behind her patted her shoulder and offered her a piece of gum. Hyacinth gave a weak smile and took it, but it didn't take away the sore bottom and the scared I-just-fell-down feeling in her chest. She bravely wiped a tear off her cheek and leaned into her mother's hug.

"How do you know I'm too old for the children's story?" Hyacinth asked her brother. "I still like going up!"

"You're too old when falling down in the aisle isn't cute anymore," Nolan replied and Hyacinth had to think about that. Perhaps, he was right. If she was old enough for "lady" shoes, perhaps she was old enough to stay in the pew too.

Mrs. Raju was just starting the story, and Hyacinth, dreading the worst, listened carefully.

"There once was a squirrel that wanted a nut," Mrs. Raju began. "He wanted it very badly!"

"See?" whispered Hyacinth. "It's a story about a squirrel!"

"I guess so," Nolan said, sounding disappointed.

Hyacinth looked at the bulletin and saw that the next thing was her father's sermon.

"Daddy's up next!" Hyacinth whispered to her mother. "I'm going to try and make him smile at me!"

And so for the rest of the service, Hyacinth did her very best to get her father to smile at her. And she managed to— once! He gave her a great big smile, and even a little chuckle! But then he forgot his place in his sermon and had to clear his throat and turn back to his notes on the podium. Hyacinth felt a little bit bad, then, but she still liked to get her father to smile at her. It was the best part of church!

"You'd think he'd be used to it by now," Mrs. Pipsner whispered. "You do this to him every week!"

"I know!" Hyacinth whispered back.

"Well, you stop now," her mother said with a wink. "Now it's my turn!"

Poor Pastor Pipsner. It was amazing that he managed to get through any sermons at all!

Chapter 8

Thanksgiving was fast approaching. Hyacinth knew this because Mrs. Raju had put up all sorts of Thanksgiving decorations. There were pumpkins, gourds, the little bouquets of wheat, and the funny cone-shaped baskets that had wax fruit spilling out. Hyacinth wondered why fruit always had to spill from baskets. If it were up to her, she would use sensible baskets that didn't spill the fruit to begin with! Maybe even baskets with lids. And little tags that told you what was inside.

"Today, children, we will all make hand turkeys!" Mrs. Raju said.

·· Hyacinth Doesn't Go to Jail ··

Hyacinth was familiar with hand turkeys. She had made one last year in grade one. It was a Thanksgiving tradition of Mrs. Raju's class. A hand turkey was made by drawing an outline of your hand, and then decorating it to look like a turkey. The thumb was the turkey's head, and the other fingers were the turkey's feathers. But this year, Hyacinth decided, she would make the best hand turkey ever. There would be no fumbling or spilled glue like in grade one. This hand turkey would be a work of art!

"Don't forget to give your turkeys feet!" Mrs. Raju reminded the class.

Hyacinth looked down at her hand outline. *Yes, feet are just what it needs!* She carefully drew some feet sticking out the bottom.

"How many toes do turkeys have?" Hyacinth asked.

"I don't know," said Ruby. "Maybe three?"

"Maybe more?" asked Hyacinth. She added more toes.

"I think three," said Ruby.

Hyacinth added two more toes to each foot and looked down at them thoughtfully. It still didn't seem right. Maybe more? She added another two to each foot. Still not right! What was going wrong?

"Mrs. Raju?" Hyacinth said, raising her hand.

"Yes, Hyacinth?" Mrs. Raju called.

"May I get a drink of water?"

Hand turkeys could be thirsty business!

"All right," Mrs. Raju said.

"Do I need a buddy?" Hyacinth asked.

"Not if you use the fountain outside our door, Hyacinth," Mrs. Raju said.

"Are you sure?" Hyacinth asked.

"Yes, Hyacinth. Now go get your drink quickly," Mrs. Raju said firmly.

Hyacinth shrugged her shoulders, stood up, and took one last long look at the turkey's toes. With a sigh, she went to the door, opened it, and walked out into the hallway.

The fountain was not far from the classroom door. Hyacinth pushed the button and watched the arch of water splash into the drain. Then she took a big, long slurp.

"Fatty!" she heard a voice say behind her. "Fatty! Fatty two by four! Can't fit through the kitchen door!"

Hyacinth was appalled! That wasn't very nice at all! Why would anyone say such a nasty thing to her? She let go of the button and turned around. She was ready to give whoever it was a piece of her mind! But she stopped.

A little way down the hall, she saw the grade four bully. He was laughing and pointing—at Nolan! Hyacinth gasped. How dare he talk like that to her brother? Nolan wasn't fat! He just wasn't skinny.

"Leave me alone," Nolan muttered.

"What did you say?" the bully asked, his voice menacing. "Say it again, fatty!"

"I said leave me alone!"

"First, say that you're a fatty!" the bully said, laughing. "Say it!"

Nolan glared up at the bully, but he was silent.

"Say it!" the bully ordered, and he pushed Nolan once, then again.

"Hey!" Hyacinth said.

The bully and Nolan looked up, both looking surprised.

"Look!" the bully said. "It's a baby!"

"I'm no baby!" said Hyacinth. "And you're mean!"

"Look, fatty, a baby has come to stand up for you!" the bully laughed.

"Go back to class, Hyacinth," Nolan said.

"No!" said Hyacinth. "That boy is mean! And he stole my eraser too!"

"Your brother's really fat, baby," the bully said, wrinkling his nose and starting to laugh again. "Look at him! You must feel awful having such a fat brother!"

Hyacinth looked at Nolan, and she saw something that gave her the strength of fourteen lions! Nolan stood there, his head hanging down, and his shoulders slumped. His eyes looked sad, and she thought she could see tears rising up in them! That big, mean bully was making her brother cry! The very thought made Hyacinth want to cry too.

"He's not fat!" Hyacinth snapped. "You're just jealous because nobody likes you."

The bully reached out and pushed Nolan, making him stumble backwards.

"That's it!" said Hyacinth, and she marched forward and kicked the bully square in the shin!

She didn't mean to kick him as hard as she did, but she was awfully angry. She felt her running shoe connect with the bully's leg, and she saw the bully's face get all red, and his eyes get all squinty.

Oh dear! she thought. *He's going to explode!*

But the bully didn't explode! He did something altogether different. *He* started to cry! His nose started to run, his eyes got all teary, and he let out a sound that sounded very much like a *boohoo!*

"You shouldn't have done that!" Nolan gasped.

Hyacinth looked at the bawling bully, and realized that she really *shouldn't* have done that! She had kicked that boy hard, and when he pulled up his pant leg to look, she could see a big red mark.

"You hurt me!" the bully cried. "That hurt!"

"You were mean to my brother!" Hyacinth declared.

"What is going on out here?" Mrs. Raju asked, as she opened the classroom door.

"That girl kicked me!" the bully wailed. "Really hard!"

"He was being mean to my brother!" Hyacinth repeated.

"She just came up and kicked me," the bully cried. "I think she broke my leg!"

"I did not!" Hyacinth said.

"You didn't kick him?" Mrs. Raju asked, frowning.

"I did kick him," Hyacinth said. "But I didn't break his leg!"

"What happened, Nolan?" Mrs. Raju asked.

"I could have kicked him myself," Nolan muttered.

"Well," Mrs. Raju said. "This is not going to be solved in the hallway. There are classes that need to continue."

"You're right, Mrs. Raju," Hyacinth sighed. "I'll go back in now. My hand turkey needs to be finished."

"I'm sorry, Hyacinth," Mrs. Raju said firmly.

Hyacinth looked up in surprise.

"What do you mean?" Hyacinth asked.

"Kicking people is not a way to solve anything! All three of you will be going to the principal's office so he can sort this out. Follow me," Mrs. Raju said.

Hyacinth's heart nearly stopped beating. She looked at Mrs. Raju in horror. *The principal's office? I'm being sent to the principal's office? That is one step before jail!*

But Mrs. Raju didn't look like she was joking—not one little bit!

Chapter 9

"The principal's office?" Hyacinth whispered to Nolan as they marched down the long hallway. "What do we do?"

"Well, you can't kick *him*!" Nolan said.

"I know," Hyacinth sighed. She was beginning to think that this was going to be a very bad day, indeed!

The principal's office was stuffy and warm. It smelled like warm-photocopied pages. The secretary was talking on the phone, her voice quiet and cheerful. She hung up and glanced at the three children and the teacher.

"Hello, Mrs. Raju," she said with a smile. "Hello, children. What can I do for you?"

"These children need to be seen by Mr. Gregory," Mrs. Raju said. "We have a situation to sort out."

"Ah," the secretary said, giving Mrs. Raju a knowing nod. "I'll see if he's free."

The secretary poked her head into another door, and then turned back and nodded. "No time like the present," she said.

Hyacinth sighed. She had been hoping that the principal would be too busy to see them, and they could all go back to class.

Mrs. Raju spoke quietly with Mr. Gregory for a few minutes. Then she said, "I must go back to class now. I have told Mr. Gregory what happened, and he will speak with you."

Hyacinth watched Mrs. Raju leave. *Oh, dear,* she thought. *At least Nolan is here!*

Mr. Gregory was a very tall man with wispy brown hair that flopped over the top of his head, almost covering his bald spot. He had thick glasses and a neat little mustache. He sat back in his chair, made a tent out of his fingers, and nodded his head even though he wasn't agreeing with anything that Hyacinth could see.

"Come in, children," Mr. Gregory said. "Sit down, please."

They did as they were told and were silent except for the bully's moans and sighs.

"Well now," Mr. Gregory asked. "What happened?"

"She kicked me," the bully said, "and I have a bruise!"

"Is that true?" Mr. Gregory asked.

"Yes," said Hyacinth.

"Did you see Hyacinth kick Clarence?" Mr. Gregory asked Nolan.

"Sure," Nolan said. "It was a great kick! I was impressed!"

"And are you sorry for kicking Clarence?" Mr. Gregory asked Hyacinth.

"Nope," Hyacinth answered.

"Hmm," said Mr. Gregory. "Then we seem to have a problem."

"She doesn't normally do this kind of thing," Nolan offered.

"She's dangerous!" the bully exclaimed.

"Clarence, I do believe there is more to the story," Mr. Gregory said pointedly. "Why did you kick Clarence, Hyacinth?"

"Because he was being mean to my brother," Hyacinth declared, "and I'm not sorry at all!"

"Is that true, Nolan?" Mr. Gregory asked.

Nolan shrugged uncomfortably.

"He's awful!" Hyacinth said. "He calls names, and he pushes. He's not nice to anyone. He took my beautiful unicorn eraser. We call him the grade four bully."

"Hyacinth," Mr. Gregory said seriously, "after today, people might call you the grade two bully!"

"That wouldn't be nice," Hyacinth said primly. "Not nice at all."

"Are you sorry that you hurt Clarence as much as you did?" Mr. Gregory asked.

"Nope," Hyacinth answered.

"Should we pray together?" Mr. Gregory asked.

"I'm not sorry," Hyacinth said, tears coming to her eyes. "I won't pray to be forgiven! I won't! I'd do it again! He was mean, and I'm not sorry!"

"Then it appears we have reached an impasse," Mr. Gregory said.

"Does that mean I can go finish my hand turkey?" Hyacinth asked.

"No, that means we will call your mother," Mr. Gregory answered.

Hyacinth watched as Mr. Gregory left his office to go make the dreaded phone call. She had never disobeyed before—not like this! But she just couldn't say she was sorry when she wasn't! It wasn't fair that she was the one getting in trouble when the bully wasn't! It wasn't fair at all! Very likely she would go to jail, and she would have the nickname, the Grade Two Bully. A tear slipped down her cheek.

"You shouldn't be crying!" the bully said. "You don't have a big bruise on your leg!"

"I should be crying!" Hyacinth exclaimed. "I have a beautiful hand turkey that won't be finished now! And it really is beautiful—"

"What about my bruise?" asked the bully.

"What about my brother?" Hyacinth asked. "What about the other kids you are always mean to?"

"So?" he said.

"You're mean," Hyacinth said, "and I might be getting in trouble, but I'm not scared of you!"

She looked at Nolan. He was watching her with a little smile on his face.

"Am I going to be locked up, Nolan?" she asked him.

"You deserve it," he said, but he gave her a grin.

The principal poked his head back in the door.

"Nolan, you may go back to class now," Mr. Gregory said.

Hyacinth settled in to wait for her mother to arrive. Her mother would not be happy about this, Hyacinth was sure. She'd never been in so much trouble in her life!

She glanced at the bully.

"So what happens to us now?" she asked.

"Don't know," the bully shrugged. "Our mothers come."

"I'm not saying I'm sorry," Hyacinth said. "But I wish the bruise weren't so big—"

Clarence looked down at his leg and frowned. "You kick pretty good for a girl," he said.

"I should take up soccer!" Hyacinth said thoughtfully. "Maybe they play soccer in jail and it can pass the time—"

"Jail?" the bully asked.

"Clarence," Hyacinth said primly. "I hate to be the first one to tell you this, but you will likely spend a great deal of time behind bars with your attitude."

And she gave him a small, sad smile.

Chapter 10

Mrs. Pipsner held the steering wheel with two hands. Her lips were pressed together in a thin line, and every couple of minutes she would sigh and shake her head. Hyacinth sat silently in the front seat, looking out the window at the rain drumming against the glass.

"Are you mad?" Hyacinth asked.

"I'm thinking, Hyacinth," her mother said.

That *wasn't* a good sign. Her mother "thought" about all sorts of things, but normally they weren't pleasant. She thought for quite some time when Hyacinth opened her birthday present before her birthday. After her mother finished thinking, she returned the present and Hyacinth didn't get it after all. Her mother thought when Hyacinth made a big mess in the kitchen, and then decided that Hyacinth and Nolan should help clean the kitchen every night after supper. And now she was thinking about Hyacinth kicking the bully. Really, this was not good at all! Thinking always brought consequence and lectures.

Hyacinth looked back at the rain on the glass. Right this very minute, her class would be finishing their hand turkeys. They would be gluing construction paper feathers to the fingers. They would be coloring turkey beaks and wattles. They would be adding stickers and glitter. Mrs. Raju would be helping the grade ones to write their names on the bottom of their pages, with their ages printed beside. This was for their mothers, who would put the picture on the refrigerator and keep it forever! But Hyacinth would not have a hand turkey this year with her age, six and three-quarters, written beside it. No, this year, she was being sent home from school for being bad.

Finally, her mother spoke, "Hyacinth, I'm proud of you."

"What?" Hyacinth thought she was dreaming.

"I am!" her mother said. "I'm very proud of you."

"For what?" Hyacinth was really puzzled.

"For standing up for your brother," her mother said. "When I was a little girl, there was a big girl who used to bully me. She was so mean. I hated going to school because I knew she would be there and she would pick on me."

"Really?" Hyacinth couldn't imagine her mother being a little girl. She couldn't imagine anyone daring to pick on her mother!

"Being picked on is terrible," Mrs. Pipsner said. "And it's good when someone stands up for someone else who is being picked on. It takes away the bully's power."

"I could kick him again tomorrow!" Hyacinth offered.

"No!" her mother said, and gave Hyacinth's leg a playful swat. "No more kicking, young lady!"

"Really, the grade four bully has been terrible," Hyacinth said. "He's so mean to everyone. He steals people's things and makes them give him their desserts. He pushes kids down too."

"What did he do to Nolan?" her mother asked.

"He called him 'fatty' and pushed him," Hyacinth said. "I wouldn't have kicked him, but Nolan looked like he wanted to cry, and then I wanted to cry, and then—well—I did it."

"Poor Nolan," Mrs. Pipsner sighed. "That was very mean!"

"So I wasn't bad after all?" Hyacinth asked.

"Well, yes and no," Mrs. Pipsner said. "You shouldn't have kicked that boy, but you were right for standing up for Nolan. That's what a good sister does."

"I don't get it," Hyacinth said mournfully. "Everyone is all mad at me for kicking the bully, but no one is mad at the bully for being mean to Nolan!"

"Kicking or hitting doesn't solve anything," Mrs. Pipsner said. "It causes more problems. Don't you see? The bully was mean, but now everyone feels sorry for him because of his big bruise."

"So what was I supposed to do?" asked Hyacinth.

"It's not easy to deal with bullies," her mother said. "But the best thing to do is to tell a teacher right away. And to stand up to him and tell him you aren't scared of him and he should stop being mean!"

"I did that," Hyacinth said, smiling to herself.

"That's why I'm proud of you," her mother said. "More kids should be as brave as you!"

"So I don't get punished?" Hyacinth asked.

"I'm still thinking," her mother replied.

"Oh, dear," Hyacinth sighed.

That evening, after more discussions about her words being more powerful than kicks to the shins, Pastor and Mrs. Pipsner finally let the matter rest.

"She has a really good kick!" Nolan said. "She should consider playing football or something! You should have seen her wind up!"

"Nolan!" Mrs. Pipsner said. "Stop that!"

"Just saying," Nolan said.

"I didn't get to finish my hand turkey," Hyacinth said.

"Is that your Thanksgiving craft from school?" Pastor Pipsner asked.

"Yes," Hyacinth said mournfully.

"How about helping me make pumpkin pies for our Thanksgiving dinner this weekend?" Pastor Pipsner asked.

"Could I put a handprint in one?" Hyacinth asked.

"No!" everyone said at once.

"Fine." Hyacinth sighed her biggest sigh. "But what is Thanksgiving with no handprints?"

Chapter 11

"I think I'm sick!" Hyacinth announced the next morning.

"Come here," Pastor Pipsner said. He put one of his big hands on Hyacinth's forehead.

"Is she sick?" Mrs. Pipsner asked.

"You don't have a fever," Pastor Pipsner said.

"Well, my stomach feels funny," Hyacinth said.

"Funny like you are going to throw up?" Pastor Pipsner asked.

Hyacinth tipped her head to one side and tested how she felt by imagining throwing up. No, that didn't seem to be it.

"Not really," she said.

"Could it be that you are nervous about going to school today?" Pastor Pipsner asked.

"Maybe," she admitted.

"Why are you nervous about school?" asked her mother. "Are you afraid of Clarence?"

"Oh, no," Hyacinth said.

"Then why are you nervous?" Pastor Pipsner asked.

Hyacinth dug her toe into the carpet and sighed. Her parents looked at her silently, both of them bent just a little bit at the waist, their eyes fixed on her.

"Well," Hyacinth said, "I got in lots of trouble yesterday— and Mrs. Raju was mad at me!"

"Ah!" said her mother. "I understand."

"You do?" Pastor Pipsner merely looked confused.

"Mrs. Raju won't like me anymore!" Hyacinth said, her voice quivering with tears. "I'm a bad kid now, and she won't like me!"

"Sure she will!" Nolan said. "You didn't kick *her*, did you?"

And Hyacinth couldn't help but laugh.

That morning, when Hyacinth walked into the grade one and two classroom, all the kids stopped talking and looked at her, wide-eyed. Hyacinth cleared her throat and walked to her desk. She stood beside it for a moment and then sat down.

"Dear God, this is terrible!" she prayed. "Just terrible!"

"What was it like?" Ruby whispered.

"What?" Hyacinth asked.

"The principal's office!" Ruby whispered louder. "What was it like?"

"Kind of stuffy," Hyacinth said, "but Mr. Gregory is nice."

"What did he do to you?" Ruby asked.

The other kids were coming closer now, and Hyacinth couldn't help but smile. She wasn't all alone after all!

"He lectured me," Hyacinth admitted, "and called my mother."

The kids gasped.

"What did your mother do?" Carl asked.

"She lectured me again, and she's still thinking—"

"About what?" asked Ruby.

"She thinks when she's really upset or not sure how to deal with us," Hyacinth said.

"Oh, you're in trouble then!" Lisa said.

"Yeah," Hyacinth agreed. "I'll probably be doing dishes and cleaning bathrooms for the rest of my life! My one comfort is that I'm pretty sure she loves me too much to send me to jail."

"All right, children," Mrs. Raju said. "Let's all go back to our seats. Let's begin our day!"

The kids went back to their seats, and Mrs. Raju read a worship story and had prayer. The first subject was math; and while they got out their workbooks, Mrs. Raju wrote some problems on the board.

"Hey, Hyacinth!" Carl whispered.

Hyacinth looked over.

"What did you do to the bully?" he asked, his eyes bright.

"Not the right thing!" Hyacinth whispered back.

"But *what*?" he insisted.

"Children!" Mrs. Raju said. "We need to stay focused. No more whispering!"

Hyacinth turned her attention back to the problems. The first one was

$$8 + 5 + 4 + 1 = \underline{\hspace{2cm}}.$$

Hyacinth sighed. This was a hard one!

"Ruby," Hyacinth whispered.

"Yes?" Ruby asked.

"Did you finish your hand turkey?" Hyacinth asked.

"Uh-huh," said Ruby. "My mom put it on the fridge."

"Man," Hyacinth said, "mine was going to be extra marvelous!"

"What were you going to do?" Ruby asked.

"Well," Hyacinth said, "I was going to—"

"Hyacinth!" Mrs. Raju said. "That's enough!"

"Mrs. Raju?" Ruby said, raising her hand.

"Yes, Ruby?" said Mrs. Raju.

"Hyacinth didn't get to finish her hand turkey," Ruby said. "And it's hard to think about math when you're thinking about the hand turkey you never got to finish."

"That's true," Mrs. Raju said. "I'll tell you what, Hyacinth. You may finish your hand turkey today after you finish your schoolwork. So the more quickly you do your math problems, the quicker you can work on your art project."

Hyacinth gave Mrs. Raju the biggest smile her face would stretch into. She had never added sums so fast in her entire life!

After school that day, Hyacinth looked down at her hand turkey. It was magnificent! It had feathers of colored construction paper, eyes of glitter, a red wattle, and her name printed across the bottom of the page: "Hyacinth Gail Pipsner." Her whole name fit this time, and it was only her age that was squished into one corner: "6 ¾." Hyacinth still thought that the number of turkey toes seemed wrong, but what could she do? She added another two toes on each foot. No, it still wasn't right.

How many toes did a turkey have, anyhow?

"Hyacinth?" Mrs. Raju called. "Do you have a minute

before you need to catch your bus?"

"Yes," said Hyacinth, and she went to Mrs. Raju's desk.

"You had a tough day yesterday," Mrs. Raju said.

"Yes," Hyacinth said with a sigh.

"Well, I wanted you to know that I am very happy to have you in my class again this year, Hyacinth," Mrs. Raju said.

Hyacinth beamed.

"You are a very creative young lady," Mrs. Raju said, "and I have an idea."

"Really?" said Hyacinth.

"Sometimes, creative people have lots of things to say," Mrs. Raju said.

"Do we ever!" Hyacinth sighed, "And it's so hard *not* to say it!"

"Well, I have a little book for you," Mrs. Raju said. "It's called a journal because it is full of empty pages. And every time you have something to say but it isn't the right time to say it, I want you to write it in this book!"

"What kinds of things?" Hyacinth asked.

"Anything you want!" said Mrs. Raju. "You could write your thoughts and feelings,

things that happened that day, things you wish, prayers. You could even write down how to deal with bullies without kicking them!"

Hyacinth looked down at the little book. Its cover had flowers on it, and there was a space at the bottom for Hyacinth to write her name. It was the most beautiful book Hyacinth had ever seen!

"Oh, Mrs. Raju!" Hyacinth said, tears coming to her eyes. "I love you!"

"Hurry, or you'll miss your bus!" Mrs. Raju said, and she gave Hyacinth a wink.

What to Do About Bullies

what Mom and Dad told me after I kicked Clarence.

- don't hitt or kick!
- pray four them.
- BE kind to them. It's hard to be mean to a kind person.
- Ignore them or walk or run away.
- Look them straight in the eye and say "leave me alone."
- stay with youre buddy. It is harder to bully two people.
- get help. If the bully just doesn't stopp, call a grown up like Mrs. Raju or Mr. Gregory or Mom or Dad.

Chapter 12

Hyacinth put her hand turkey on the fridge and stood back to admire it. It was truly the best hand turkey that had ever been made in all of Highview Christian Academy!

"Hey, Nolan, look at my hand turkey!" Hyacinth said.

"How many toes does that thing have?" Nolan asked, looking closer.

"Nevermind that!" Hyacinth said. "Isn't it gorgeous?"

"It's pretty nice," Nolan agreed, and Hyacinth smiled in satisfaction.

"Time to help, kids!" Pastor Pipsner said, and he handed

Hyacinth a stack of plates and Nolan some cutlery. "The Thanksgiving table needs to be set!"

As Hyacinth and Nolan put the plates in front of the chairs and the forks and knives around the plates, the smell of Thanksgiving dinner filled the house. There would be yams, stuffing, peas, and creamy mashed potatoes. There would be vegetarian roast and nut gravy to drizzle on top. And there would be pumpkin pie for dessert.

"Mommy!" Hyacinth called. "We need candles!"

"We do?" she called back.

"Yep!" Hyacinth hollered. "To make it special!"

When Mrs. Pipsner arrived with candles, Hyacinth leaned her elbows on the table and watched while her father struck a match and lit them. The little flames flickered and danced. Hyacinth sighed with happiness. This would be just perfect!

"Let's eat!" Pastor Pipsner said. "Sit down, everyone!"

Hyacinth clambered into her chair and picked up her fork so that she would be ready.

"Fork down, Miss," Pastor Pipsner said. "First things first."

"Grace?" Nolan asked.

"Before that," Pastor Pipsner said, and Nolan moaned. "But I'm starving!" he said.

"First," Pastor Pipsner said, "I want everyone to think of something they are thankful for."

Hyacinth looked down at the gleaming white plate. She looked at the mounds of creamy mashed potatoes and the vegetarian roast with the spoon stuck in the middle. She looked at her father with his happy eyes and at her mother with her pretty smile. She looked at Nolan who was eyeing the yams like a ferocious wolf.

"I'm thankful for my family," Pastor Pipsner said. "I'm thankful for my beautiful wife and for my two kids. What are you thankful for, Mommy?"

"Well," Mrs. Pipsner said, "I'm thankful for food on our table, a roof over our heads, and a whole day to spend together. What are you thankful for, Nolan?"

"What?" Nolan pulled his eyes away from the food and snatched his hand back from the mashed potatoes.

"What are you thankful for?" Mrs. Pipsner asked.

"I'm thankful that Hyacinth isn't in jail yet!" he said.

"Hey!" said Hyacinth, but her parents just laughed.

"What are you thankful for, Hyacinth?" asked Pastor Pipsner.

Hyacinth thought for a moment. She thought about grade two, about hand turkeys, math problems, bullies, and new best friends. She thought about brothers, mothers, fathers, and the dog she wished she had. She thought about all the things she wanted to say but couldn't fit them all in before the food got cold!

"I'm thankful for the journal Mrs. Raju gave me," Hyacinth said. "You know why?"

"Why?" her mother asked.

"Because it will never tell me to be quiet!" she said.

"Thank You for the food we eat," the family said together. "Thank You for the world so sweet. Thank You for the birds that sing. Thank You, God, for everything! Amen."

"Pass the potatoes, please," said Nolan.

dear God,

I love my grandma!!! thank You that I can call her any time I want because of our good long distance plan!

My grandma has wrinkels. She has lots of gray hair too. I like that. I like how she smells like flowers and powder too. When I ~~grown~~ grow up I hope I have lots of wrinkles like Grandma. Mommy says that her job gives her wrinkles. she must like her job a lott because wrinkles are pretty!!

well anyway God. I just wanted to say thank You ~~four~~ for making Grandma all wrinkly and kind. I love her. please give her more wrinkles.

and please give me a dog.

most Sincerely,

Hyacinth Gail Pipsner

Book 2

Hyacinth Doesn't Miss Christmas

Chapter 1

Hyacinth Gail Pipsner was six and three-quarters years old and in grade two. She was not nervous at all about grade two because, after all, she had done grade one the year before and school was not new to her. Besides, she had the same teacher as last year, Mrs. Raju, who taught grades one and two together.

On this particular morning, the Monday after Thanksgiving, Mrs. Raju's grade one and two class was all abuzz.

"Now class!" Mrs. Raju called. "We are going to talk about what we did for Thanksgiving. I will ask each of you what food you had for Thanksgiving dinner, and write it on the board. Who would like to go first?"

"Tofu turkey!" someone said.

"Stuffing!" said someone else.

"Cake!" said someone else.

Hyacinth raised her hand and hopped in her seat. Mrs. Raju had told her to write her thoughts and to be quiet in class. Hyacinth was not about to disappoint Mrs. Raju, especially since she had given Hyacinth such a beautiful journal. So Hyacinth hopped in her seat and waved her hand wildly, waiting to be called.

"Lisa?" Mrs. Raju said.

"Roast!" said Lisa.

That was what Hyacinth was going to say. She sighed and tried to think of something else.

"Erwin?" Mrs. Raju called next.

"Potatoes!" said Erwin.

Oh, he had taken that one too!

"Veggies!"

"Pickles!"

"Pie!"

What was left? If Mrs. Raju had only called on her earlier, Hyacinth was sure she would have had a wonderful answer.

"Hyacinth?" Mrs. Raju said. "You have been very patient. What can you think of from Thanksgiving dinner?"

And Hyacinth could not think of anything. Not one thing! It had all been said.

"Roast?" Hyacinth said weakly.

"I already said that!" Lisa said, smiling proudly, her white, white socks glowing over her indoor running shoes.

"Well, our roast was special!" Hyacinth declared.

"How was it special?" Mrs. Raju asked.

"It was exotic," Hyacinth said. "My father made it out of puffed rice cereal and cottage cheese. I think that recipe is from my father's Russian heritage."

"Oh, we make that kind all the time," Lisa said. "Everybody does! It's nothing special."

"Do you roast ants and grasshoppers for a crunchy topping?" Hyacinth asked.

"No," Lisa said, looking a little sick.

Hyacinth gave a small smile and folded her hands in front of her on her desk, looking forward. She was finished now.

"Hyacinth," Mrs. Raju said. "Did *you* roast ants and grasshoppers for a crunchy topping to your roast?"

"No," Hyacinth sighed, "but I didn't have anything special to say."

Mrs. Raju quickly changed the subject. "All of the words on the blackboard are going to be our spelling list for this week. Write them down carefully so that you can learn how to spell them."

Hyacinth slid down in her desk so she could look inside. She pulled out her spelling notebook and her pencil. It was covered with teeth marks and the eraser was chewed off. Hyacinth began to write down the words on the board: *Tofu turkey, stuffing, potatoes.*

"Hyacinth!"

Hyacinth turned to see Ruby, and she gave her friend a sad smile.

"We had roast too," Ruby said. "I love roast!"

Hyacinth grinned.

"I have something for you," Ruby said. "It's a present!"

"What is it?" Hyacinth whispered back.

"I can't say," Ruby replied. "It's a surprise!"

Ruby ducked down behind her desk where Hyacinth couldn't see. She *heard* the sound of crumpling paper. Then Ruby popped up with a little present wrapped like a candy, twisted at both ends.

As Hyacinth unwrapped her present, a little piece of paper fell out that read

To Hyacinth
From, ~~your friend,~~
Your best friend,
Ruby Alice Marie McDonald

And inside the lined wrapping paper was a brand-new bottle of pearly pink nail polish. Hyacinth gasped. It was such a pretty color. She had never owned nail polish before. Not ever! That was because Hyacinth was not allowed to wear nail polish. But now, quite accidentally, Hyacinth was the owner of a brand-new bottle of pearly pink nail polish.

"Thank you!" Hyacinth whispered. "I'm not allowed to wear it, though."

"Maybe you could save it," Ruby suggested. "Until you are allowed?"

But that would be never. Hyacinth had a better idea!

"Oh, Ruby," Hyacinth said. "I couldn't wait that long! I'd explode!"

For Thanksgiving, we didn't have roast ~~whith~~ with crunchy bug topping, but it sure sounds interesting!

Chapter 2

Melissa was the most beautiful and real looking baby doll that Hyacinth had ever owned. She felt like a real baby. She was as big as a real baby, too, and she had shining blond hair with blue eyes. She wore a real baby's diaper, and she had a real baby bottle. She wore a sleeper from when Hyacinth was a baby, so Hyacinth knew for sure that Melissa was the size of a real baby! Hyacinth had only just now noticed, however, that Melissa had a flaw. Her fingernails did not look real at all! They looked like rubber. It was not acceptable.

"What are you doing?" Nolan asked.

Hyacinth whipped the nail polish behind her back and gave her most innocent look.

"Nothing," she said.

"You looked like you were about to operate on Melissa," he said.

"I am not!" Hyacinth retorted. "I am her mother, and I would never do that!"

"Huh," said Nolan. He stood in the hallway, looking into Hyacinth's room. "So what are you doing?"

"I'm—I'm thinking!" she said.

"About what?" he asked.

"Can you keep a secret?" she asked, lowering her voice.

"Yes," Nolan said, his eyes lighting up.

"Well, I was wondering if it would be wrong to paint Melissa's nails," she said.

"You aren't allowed to have nail polish," Nolan said.

"I know!" Hyacinth said. "But what if—and I'm only saying what if—what if I had some nail polish that I would never put on my own nails? But what if Melissa's nails looked very plain and rubberlike? Then would it be wrong to use some of the nail polish on Melissa's nails? Especially if I never, ever used it again?"

Nolan shrugged his shoulders. "I don't know," he said. "You should ask Dad."

"It's a secret!" Hyacinth exclaimed.

"Oh, well then, don't ask Dad," Nolan said, shrugging again. "I thought it would be something more interesting than that—girls!"

Nolan wandered down the hallway, and Hyacinth turned back to Melissa. She carefully unscrewed the cap from the nail polish and pulled out the brush. With one quick dab, she painted one of Melissa's nails. She stood back to get a better look. Yes, it did look good. It looked so real! Hyacinth stuck her tongue out the side of her mouth and carefully, ever so carefully, painted the rest of Melissa's nails. Then she screwed the top back onto the nail polish and put it into her drawer, right in the middle of her rolled-up socks.

"This is OK, isn't it, God?" Hyacinth asked. "I'm not wearing it myself. Only Melissa is. And she is only a doll."

Hyacinth wasn't convinced that her mother would agree, and she started to feel nervous.

"Huh." Nolan had come back and was peering over Hyacinth's shoulder. "It's kind of obvious, isn't it?"

"No, it looks real!" Hyacinth said.

"Whatever," Nolan shrugged. "You know how Dad and Mom hate makeup."

"Nolan, you'd better not tell!" Hyacinth said.

"What do I care about your doll?" Nolan asked. "I don't care about dolls!"

"OK, then," Hyacinth said.

"What I do care about is dishes," Nolan said.

"What about them?" Hyacinth asked.

"I hate doing them," he replied, "and I sure wish I didn't have to do them tonight."

Hyacinth sighed a big sigh.

"OK," she said. "I'll dry them alone tonight."

That night during supper, Hyacinth couldn't help but watch every single dish that was being used.

"Are you sure you need a new spoon, Daddy?" she asked her father.

"Mine dropped!" he said.

"OK," she sighed.

And the family continued eating their bowls of lentil soup.

"We don't need plates for bread!" Hyacinth said. "The table is clean!"

"We use plates in this house, Hyacinth," her mother said.

"OK," she sighed.

And the family continued to eat their bowls of lentil soup.

"Nolan!" Hyacinth exclaimed. "You don't need to stir your juice!"

"Yes, I do!" Nolan said, dipping a fork into his juice cup. "I don't like it when the pulp all goes to the bottom!"

"Well, you don't need two plates for bread!" Hyacinth said.

"I don't want the two halves of my bread to touch," Nolan replied.

"And why are you getting a new bowl for more soup?" she demanded.

"Because this bowl is used!" Nolan retorted.

Hyacinth sighed and glared angrily across the table.

"You are very wasteful," Hyacinth said primly. "Very, very wasteful, Nolan!"

"Are you sure you don't want a plate for your bread, dear?" her mother asked.

"No, thank you," Hyacinth said, glaring angrily at her brother. "I would rather hold it."

And she did. It was one less plate she would have to dry.

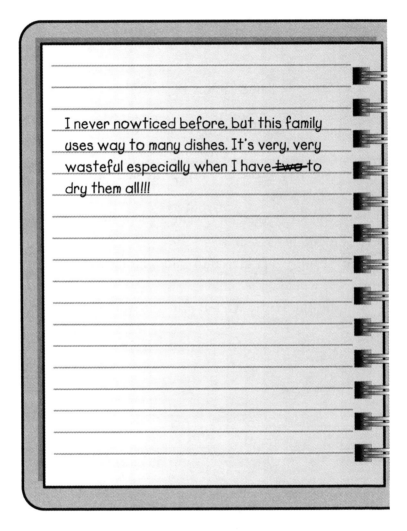

I never nowticed before, but this family uses way to many dishes. It's very, very wasteful especially when I have ~~two~~ to dry them all!!!

Chapter 3

The next day at school, Mrs. Raju told the class about Native Americans and how they used to live.

"They lived off the land," Mrs. Raju said. "Does anyone know what this means?"

"They hunted and fished!" someone said.

"And didn't waste anything!" someone else added.

"That's right!" said Mrs. Raju. "They knew how to use every part of an animal. They didn't waste any part of it. They also knew how to use plants for medicine and for food. We are going to watch a video today about the Native Americans in

North America before Europeans arrived."

The children gathered on the TV-watching mat and waited for Mrs. Raju. She put the DVD into the player, put her glasses on to look more closely, pressed a button, and waited. Nothing happened. Mrs. Raju pressed a different button and the TV came to life.

Hyacinth was perfectly amazed by the video. Imagine living without running water or heaters or grocery stores! It was more than amazing. Hyacinth decided right then and there that she wanted to be Native American too.

"I want to be a Native American princess," Hyacinth said that day at recess.

"Me too!" Ruby said.

"Let's both be princesses," Hyacinth said. "My name will be Beautiful Flower, and yours can be Liquid Sunshine."

"OK!" Ruby said. "What will we do?"

"We have to find food!" Hyacinth said.

And so Hyacinth and Ruby went in search of food. They looked around the teeter-totters and behind the swings. They looked under the jungle gym.

"We can use rocks for pretend bread," Ruby said.

"No," said Hyacinth. "We have to find real food, and make it like the Native Americans did!"

"Like what?" Ruby asked.

"I don't know," Hyacinth said, looking around. But then she saw it!

"Where are you going?" Ruby called, running after Hyacinth.

"I'm going to try this," Hyacinth said, squatting down on the sidewalk.

Ruby looked down doubtfully. "Try what?" she asked.

"This is lemon grass," Hyacinth said. "At least I think it is. I'm going to chew some and see if it tastes lemony."

"But it's growing in the sidewalk crack!" Ruby said.

"It is growing from the earth," Hyacinth said solemnly. "It is a gift from the earth, and I am going to eat it!"

"You first," Ruby said.

So Hyacinth plucked a small weed from the sidewalk crack and wiped it off on her pants. Then she popped it into her mouth and started to chew.

"What does it taste like?" Ruby asked.

"I think it tastes a little bit lemony!" Hyacinth said. "I think—"

"Let me try some," Ruby said. She plucked some and popped it into her mouth, chewing thoughtfully.

"Maybe I need to eat more of it," Hyacinth said. "It's hard to tell."

She picked another weed and popped it into her mouth, followed by another.

"This is probably very nutritious," Hyacinth said between chews. "It will keep us healthy when we live outside in our tents all winter long!"

"But we are princesses," Ruby said. "I don't want to live outside during winter."

"We are not *spoiled* princesses," Hyacinth said. "We must know how to take care of ourselves!"

"Look!" said Ruby. "If you pull on the top of the grass, it kind of slides out and there is newer grass. I'm going to taste this!"

"Let me try too!" Hyacinth said.

They were so busy sampling the delights of the sidewalk that they did not notice the shadow fall over them until it was too late. Hyacinth and Ruby looked up slowly into the curious face of Mrs. Raju.

"What are you eating, girls?" Mrs. Raju asked.

Hyacinth was silent.

"Hyacinth?" Mrs. Raju pressed. "What are you eating?"
Hyacinth pointed down. Mrs. Raju looked.

"Are you eating weeds?" Mrs. Raju asked carefully.

"We are eating the gifts of the earth," Hyacinth said proudly. "We do not eat weeds."

"Ah," Mrs. Raju said, crossing her arms over her chest. "Which weeds, exactly, did you eat?"

"Those," Ruby said, pointing.

"Ah," Mrs. Raju said. "Please spit it out, girls."

"I can't," Hyacinth said. "I swallowed."

"Come inside, you two," Mrs. Raju said. "We need to have a talk."

Hyacinth exchanged a nervous look with Ruby, but they did as they were told and trailed after Mrs. Raju back into the school. They walked down the long hallway, past the grade three and four classroom and past the bathrooms. They followed their teacher all the way to their classroom.

"Sit down, please," Mrs. Raju said.

"Are we in trouble?" Hyacinth asked.

"Why would you eat weeds, girls?" Mrs. Raju asked.

"We were being Native American princesses," Ruby said.

"I am Beautiful Flower, and Ruby is Liquid Sunshine," Hyacinth said.

"Do you know if those weeds were safe to eat?" Mrs. Raju

asked. "Do you know if they were poisonous?"

"No," Hyacinth said.

"Do you know if they were sprayed by weed killer?" Mrs. Raju asked.

"No," Ruby said.

"Girls, you must never eat anything off of the ground!" Mrs. Raju said. "Now you are going to have to stay close to me all day today so that I can watch you for any signs of sickness. And I am going to send a letter home with each of you for your parents to sign. I expect you to return them to me tomorrow."

"Yes, Mrs. Raju," Hyacinth and Ruby said together.

"I think we're safe," Hyacinth whispered to Ruby when Mrs. Raju went back to her desk to begin writing the letters.

"She's writing letters to send home with us!" Ruby exclaimed.

"I know," Hyacinth said, trying to sound braver than she felt. "But I don't feel sick, so I don't think we've been poisoned and that is good news!"

"That *is* good news," Ruby said solemnly. "If I were poisoned, my mother would kill me!"

Chapter 4

That afternoon, when Hyacinth and Nolan got home from school, Hyacinth stood for a very long time with her backpack on her back and her shoes still on her feet. Nolan kicked off his sneakers and wandered into the kitchen to find a snack, but Hyacinth still stood at the door. She was thinking.

"Hyacinth, what is wrong with you?" Nolan hollered.

"Nothing!" she hollered back.

"Then how come you aren't eating?" he called back all muffled with his mouth full of apple.

"That is a good question," Hyacinth's father, Pastor Pipsner, said. "Why aren't you, Hyacinth? Are you sick?"

"No," Hyacinth said. "I am not sick. I am very sure that I am not sick!"

Pastor Pipsner stood looking at Hyacinth, stroking his beard with one hand. Nolan came out of the kitchen and stood looking at Hyacinth. Hyacinth sighed and slowly took off her backpack.

"I had a very bad day today," Hyacinth said. She tried to look dignified but wasn't sure she managed.

"What happened?" Pastor Pipsner asked.

"This should explain it," she said, taking the letter out of her backpack. "Mrs. Raju says you have to sign it and I have to bring it back."

"Oh!" Nolan gasped.

"Oh," Pastor Pipsner said.

"Yes," said Hyacinth.

"You got a letter from your teacher?" Nolan asked in surprise. "You must have been really, really bad!"

"I wasn't!" Hyacinth said.

"Then why did she send a letter?" Nolan asked. "You probably were awful!"

"I wasn't!" Hyacinth said, her voice beginning to quaver.

"Now, now," Pastor Pipsner said. "Let's read the letter and find out."

So he opened the letter and began to read. He made a *hmfph* sound, and he frowned. He stopped reading, looked at Hyacinth, and then continued to read. When he had finished, he folded the letter up and tapped it on his hand. Then he opened it and looked at it again.

"Hyacinth," Pastor Pipsner said after a moment, "why were you eating weeds?"

"Weeds?" Nolan said.

"It isn't how it sounds!" Hyacinth exclaimed. "Did she tell you that we were being Native American princesses? Did she say that I was Beautiful Flower and Ruby was Liquid Sunshine?"

"No, she did not mention that," Pastor Pipsner said. "She did mention that the weeds were growing in a sidewalk crack—"

"The Native Americans lived off the land!" Hyacinth exclaimed. "We were living off the land!"

"You were living off of weeds!" Nolan said.

"That's enough, Nolan," Pastor Pipsner said.

"I was looking for lemon grass and I wanted to see if it tasted lemony!" Hyacinth said.

"Did it?" Nolan asked.

"A little!" Hyacinth said.

"Did you stop to think that animals go to the bathroom outside?" Pastor Pipsner said. "What if a dog or cat had gone to the bathroom on those weeds before you ate them?"

Hyacinth was silent.

"I think if a cat went to the bathroom on weeds," Nolan said quietly, "they might taste a little . . . lemony."

"Nolan!" Hyacinth said. "Stop it!"

"I'm just saying," said Nolan.

"I saw the video about Native Americans," Hyacinth said, "and they did such wonderful things like you wouldn't believe. Did you know that they traveled and hunted and knew how to make medicine out of plants?"

"Yes," said Pastor Pipsner. "But you are not a Native American and you don't know the special plants!"

"I know," Hyacinth sighed. "And it's very boring being half Russian and half French and half Scottish and half Ukrainian. Even our Thanksgiving roast wasn't something interesting!"

"Oh," said Pastor Pipsner. "Well, would you like to eat something interesting tonight for supper?"

"Not if means roasting ants," Hyacinth said, shaking her head.

Pastor Pipsner gave his daughter a funny look.

"Don't ask!" she said, throwing her hands in the air. "It was that kind of day!"

That evening after supper and after drying the dishes with Nolan, Hyacinth sat in the middle of her parents' bed, watching her mother fold laundry.

"Do you get hungry at school?" her mother asked.

"No," said Hyacinth.

"Do you get enough food in your lunch?" asked her mother.

"Yes," said Hyacinth. "I was trying to be a Native American princess. No one understands—"

"I do," her mother said with a smile.

"Really?" asked Hyacinth.

"I think so," her mother said. "I was a little girl once, too, you know."

"Did you ever pretend to be a Native American princess?" asked Hyacinth.

"I used to pretend to be a horse," said her mother.

"Ah," said Hyacinth. "What did Grandma do when you ate grass?"

"I didn't really eat the grass," her mother said. "I only pretended."

"Oh," said Hyacinth.

Hyacinth's mother picked up a towel and folded it into a neat rectangle.

"Just pretend, Hyacinth," her mother said.

As Hyacinth walked out of her parents' bedroom, she let out a big sigh. She had gotten into quite enough trouble for one day, and Melissa, with her painted nails, was still waiting to be discovered! She didn't want to get into any more trouble, and the thought of Melissa's nails being discovered was suddenly more than Hyacinth could bear.

She dashed to her room and pulled Melissa out of her cozy little baby bed. Hyacinth bent over Melissa's fingers and tried to scratch the nail polish off. But it didn't work! The nail polish didn't scratch off!

Hyacinth sat back and looked at Melissa's nails. This was not good at all! She scratched at them again. Nothing. Hyacinth bent over the nails and chewed at them with her teeth. When she looked down at Melissa's fingers, all wet with spit, Hyacinth saw that it was working!

Hyacinth chewed all the nail polish off of Melissa's nails and breathed a big sigh of relief!

She had been in enough trouble for one day!

Weeds don't taste that good especially
when you think about ware they have
been. I'm gladd I never tried ants and
grasshoppers on a roast!

~~espesally~~
~~esoepesially~~
especially

Chapter 5

It was getting quite cold in the mornings, so cold the ground was frosty when Hyacinth and Nolan waited for the bus to come. Hyacinth liked to walk through the frost on the grass and make footprints.

"It's like footprints on the moon!" Hyacinth said.

Nolan just looked down at his feet and then back down the street in the direction the bus would come from.

"Maybe we can wear our boots tomorrow!" Hyacinth said.

"I'm not wearing boots for frost!" Nolan said. "That's dumb."

"Well, I like my new winter boots," Hyacinth said. "They look like moon boots!"

"That's the problem," Nolan muttered.

"Except they are pink," Hyacinth added. "Pink moon boots. That makes them for a girl astronaut, you know. I'm sure there are girl astronauts who wear pink moon boots, Nolan."

"I'm sure there aren't!" Nolan said.

"Why not?" asked Hyacinth.

"Because astronauts are grown-up ladies, and grown-up ladies don't wear pink anymore, they wear red," he said.

"Oh," said Hyacinth. She hadn't thought of that. In her mind she saw all sorts of lady astronauts with bright red moon boots, making footprints on the moon, and she liked it.

"Are you feeling all right?" Nolan asked after a moment.

"Yes," said Hyacinth. "Why?"

"Just wondering," he said.

Hyacinth looked back down at the frost that was melting around her running shoes.

"Do you have a hot head?" he asked.

"No," she said.

"Oh, OK," Nolan said.

"Why?" asked Hyacinth.

"Just wondering," he replied.

Hyacinth looked back down at the frost and started to

make little roads in it with the toe of her shoe.

"Does your tongue feel dry?" Nolan asked.

"No!" said Hyacinth. "Why are you asking these things?"

"Because I saw you chewing on nail polish last night," Nolan said.

"So?" Hyacinth was getting annoyed now. "It just means that Melissa doesn't have nail polish on her fingers anymore and I won't get in trouble and you have to do dishes with me."

"Nail polish is poisonous, that's all," Nolan said.

"Poisonous!" Hyacinth gasped.

"Yep," Nolan said. "Poisonous. You aren't supposed to eat it."

"I didn't know!" Hyacinth wailed. "What do I do now?"

"I don't know," Nolan said. "But I'd be careful and watch for signs of poisoning if I were you."

"What are the signs?" she asked.

"A hot head," he said, "and a dry tongue. I think you might feel prickly, too, and you might get a stomachache."

Hyacinth sighed a big sigh. The last thing she needed was to be poisoned! If she was poisoned, her parents were going to be really mad! Especially after the weed-eating incident!

It was a very long bus ride to school that day. When Hyacinth finally got off the bus, she thought that her head might feel a little bit hot. Perhaps it was her big, new winter coat, but she couldn't be sure.

"Ruby!" Hyacinth said when she saw her friend. "Is my head hot?"

"I don't want to touch it," Ruby said. "It looks all hot and sticky."

"Oh, dear," Hyacinth sighed. "I think my stomach is starting to hurt."

"Did you get in trouble for eating weeds?" Ruby asked.

"Yes," said Hyacinth. "Did you?"

"Yes," said Ruby. "My mother said we'd better stop it or she'll give me spinach in my lunch for a week."

"Yuck," said Hyacinth.

"We'd better stop it, then!" Ruby said seriously. "I don't like spinach, and my mom doesn't joke about stuff like that!"

That morning, during their spelling test, Hyacinth could not focus on spelling *tofu, turkey,* or *stuffing.* Instead, she kept thinking about her tongue. It was hard to tell if it felt dry or not. How wet did her tongue normally feel? She stuck it out and felt it with her fingers.

"Potatoes," Mrs. Raju said. "Please spell the word *potatoes.*"

Hyacinth tried to focus. P-O-T-

Hyacinth was clutching her pencil very tightly in her fingers, so tightly that her fingers began to tingle. Wasn't that a sign of poisoning too?

"Hyacinth, are you all right?" Mrs. Raju asked.

"I may be dying," Hyacinth said mournfully.

"Dying?" said Mrs. Raju. "Why?"

"My fingers are tingling," said Hyacinth.

"Anything else?" asked Mrs. Raju.

Hyacinth thought about it. Her head didn't feel hot, and her tummy was all right.

"Not right now, Mrs. Raju," Hyacinth said. "But I'll keep you posted."

"Are you really dying?" Ruby asked when they were going outside for recess.

"I can't be sure," Hyacinth said. "But I thought I should be careful, just in case."

"Well, try not to die," Ruby said. "Christmas is coming, and it would be terrible to miss it!"

Hyacinth had to agree that the timing was just terrible.

Chapter 6

That afternoon at home, Hyacinth munched halfheartedly on apple slices and cheese. When Nolan took a piece of cheese off her plate, she didn't even have the heart to demand it back.

"Don't you want your cheese?" Nolan asked in surprise.

"You can have it all," Hyacinth answered. "I'm not hungry."

"Still not hungry?" he said. "What's wrong?"

"I'm dying," she said solemnly. "It's a terrible thing to die right before Christmas. I'll miss all the fun."

"Oh, the nail polish," Nolan said, nodding.

"Yes," she said. "The nail polish. My fingers tingled earlier and my head was hot in the bus and my tongue might be dry right now, but I can't be sure because I never think about it when my tongue is wet."

"Hmm," said Nolan. "I know what you need."

"A cure?" she asked hopefully.

"Nope, a will," he said.

"What's that?" Hyacinth asked.

"It's a legal paper where you write down what you want people to have once you've died," Nolan said. "You should probably write one."

"Will you help me?" she asked.

So Hyacinth and Nolan went upstairs to Hyacinth's bedroom and sat down with a paper and pen. Hyacinth chewed on the end of the pen as she thought. She had never written a will before, and it felt very important.

"What do I say?" Hyacinth asked, after a few minutes of staring at the blank paper.

"You start by writing 'last will and testament,' " Nolan said.

Hyacinth wrote it down.

"And then you say," Nolan said, " 'I want all my things to go to—' "

"To who?" Hyacinth asked.

"Well, since I'm your brother, it would only make sense to leave them to me," Nolan answered.

"What about Mommy and Daddy?" Hyacinth asked.

"They don't play with toys anymore," Nolan pointed out.

"What about Ruby?" Hyacinth asked.

"She's not family, Hyacinth," Nolan said, shaking his head.

"Will you take care of Melissa?" Hyacinth asked.

"Of course!" Nolan said.

"OK, then," Hyacinth said. And in the space after *I want all my things to go to,* Hyacinth wrote, "Nolan."

"Now you sign it," Nolan said.

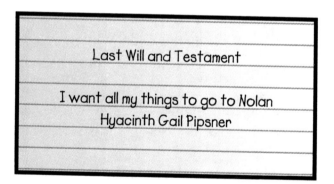

Last Will and Testament

I want all my things to go to Nolan
Hyacinth Gail Pipsner

So Hyacinth carefully wrote her entire name: *Hyacinth Gail Pipsner.* Then she laid the will on her desk where it could be found, and went to lie on her bed. She lay very still, with her arms at her sides, but that didn't seem right. So she draped one arm above her head, and that seemed much better. She let out a long sigh, just to show how very sad she was.

Hyacinth didn't hear Nolan leave, but she could hear her father cooking supper downstairs, and she could hear her mother talking on the phone. Her father was cooking lasagna, her favorite. Hyacinth was beginning to wish she had written her will after supper. She listened to the tinkling of pots and spoons. She listened to her mother laugh and say Goodbye to the person she was talking to. Hyacinth listened to the muffled sound of voices on the radio. Her dad must be listening to the news. It sounded so comfy and nice downstairs that she was almost ready to get up and go down. Just then her mother tapped on Hyacinth's door and poked her head inside.

"There you are!" her mother said. "Why are you in bed?"

"I'm waiting to die," Hyacinth said. "But it's OK because I wrote a will."

"Oh, you did?" her mother asked, picking up the paper on the desk. "It looks like Nolan will have a lot of girls' toys."

"It would mean a lot to him." Hyacinth sighed.

"And why are you dying?" her mother asked.

"Don't be mad," Hyacinth said weakly, "but it's nail polish poisoning—"

"You drank nail polish?" her mother gasped.

"No!" Hyacinth said, lifting her head. "I chewed it off of Melissa's nails!"

"Are we talking about a girl at school or your doll?" her mother asked.

"My doll," Hyacinth answered.

"Oh." Mrs. Pipsner looked relieved.

"So I must say Goodbye—" Hyacinth sighed again.

"Before lasagna?" her mother asked.

"I don't have much choice!" Hyacinth said. "I'm poisoned!"

Mrs. Pipsner sat down on Hyacinth's bed and put a cool hand on her forehead. "You aren't going to die, Hyacinth," she said with a chuckle.

"I'm not?" Hyacinth asked, opening her eyes and raising her head.

"Not tonight, sweetheart," her mother said.

"Are you sure?" asked Hyacinth.

"Positive," her mother said. "But I think we should talk about something."

Hyacinth sat up and smiled to herself. She did feel much better, now that she thought about it! She felt downright hungry!

"Chewing dried nail polish won't poison you," her mother said. "But you do seem to be eating an awful lot of things that aren't food lately."

"I know."

"And some things *are* poisonous," her mother said. "You might not know it, though."

"How do I know?" Hyacinth asked.

"I'll tell you what," her mother replied. "Stick to the things I pack in your lunch or put on the table."

"Hmm," Hyacinth said.

"And if you happen to eat something else that doesn't fit those requirements, I want you to tell an adult right away!" her mother said. "Do you understand?"

"Yes," Hyacinth answered.

"I'm serious about this, Hyacinth," her mother said. "No more eating things that aren't food!"

"OK," Hyacinth agreed.

"Now, show me the nail polish," her mother said.

Hyacinth slowly got up off the bed and opened her sock drawer.

"Let's go have supper!" her mother said. "And this," she picked up the bottle of nail polish, "belongs to me now."

today, I wrote my "last will and testa-
mint." I left everything to Nolan. He
promised to take care of Melissa.
   mom says I'm not going to die because
of the nail polish. since she took it, I
guess I won't for sure. Mom said to stick
with the food she ~~pake~~ packs in my lunch
or puts on the table. I hope she putts
lots of Dad's lassagne on the table. It's
yummy!!

Chapter 7

Hyacinth was very grateful not to be poisoned, and so she decided that it would be proper to write a psalm. Psalms were prayers that King David wrote to God, and Hyacinth thought that she should do the same thing.

So the next afternoon, she sat down with her journal for all her thoughts that Mrs. Raju had given her and a pen. The pen was a purple pen, so it was extra special.

dear God,

thank You for letting me not be poisoned. I'm very happy to be alive! Thank
You for not ~~ledding~~ letting the nail polish kill
me like Nolan said.

I think You're great. and I'm going to try
very hard to be good from now on. I've
been kind of bad the last little while. You
~~mite~~ might have noticed.

So thank You for letting me live!

Yours truely,
Hyacinth Gail Pipsner

Yes, it seemed just right! Hyacinth felt much better having written her psalm, and she carefully closed her book.

"What are you doing?" Nolan asked.

"Nothing!" said Hyacinth. "It's private!"

"But the book is mine," Nolan said.

"No, it's not!" Hyacinth said. "Mrs. Raju gave it to me!"

"But you willed it to me," Nolan said.

"I didn't die!" Hyacinth replied.

"That doesn't matter," Nolan said. "A will is a legal document.

It doesn't matter if you are dead or not. When you wrote the will, you gave all of your things to me!"

Hyacinth was stunned! This couldn't be!

"But what about Melissa?" Hyacinth asked.

"Mine," Nolan said.

"My bed?" asked Hyacinth.

"Mine," said Nolan.

"My backpack and my pink moon boots?" asked Hyacinth.

"Mine too," said Nolan. "Look, Hya-Bya, I'm sorry about this. But the law is the law!"

"Oh, dear," Hyacinth sighed.

"It could be worse," Nolan said. "You could have willed your things to Ruby, and a truck would be taking them away right now."

"That's true," Hyacinth said.

"I'll tell you what," Nolan said. "I can't sleep in two beds, so I'll let you sleep in the one that used to be yours. And you can still sleep in the room that used to be yours, too, if you want."

"That's nice!" Hyacinth said. "Thanks, Nolan!"

"But if you could just ask me before you use my things—" he said.

"OK," Hyacinth said weakly. "I could do that—"

"Good," said Nolan. "See you!"

·· Hyacinth Doesn't Miss Christmas ··

Hyacinth watched as Nolan walked out of the room. This was not good! She wished she had thought ahead before writing the will, but now it was done and Nolan owned all of her things!

Hyacinth looked at Melissa in her little bed and felt a wave of sadness. Poor Melissa! Hyacinth had loved her dearly, but now Melissa was not hers anymore. Poor Melissa belonged to Nolan, who would not be a very attentive parent at all.

"Nolan!" Hyacinth called.

Nolan poked his head back into the room.

"Can I play with Melissa?" Hyacinth asked.

"I suppose so," Nolan said.

Hyacinth picked up Melissa and rocked her gently back and forth.

"I'm sorry, Melissa," Hyacinth whispered. "This didn't turn out the way it was supposed to at all!"

That evening, as Pastor Pipsner was choosing something to read for evening worship, Mrs. Pipsner looked out the big living room window.

"Is that snow I see?" she asked.

Hyacinth and Nolan ran to the window to look, and sure enough, big, fluffy flakes of snow were falling outside in the darkness. They swirled and danced. Hyacinth squinted and looked as far as she could, there were still more flakes coming and coming. It was beautiful!

"Oh, wow!" Hyacinth said. "Snow!"

"I wonder if there will be enough to go sledding!" Nolan said.

"Let's go outside and play in it now!" Hyacinth said.

"No, no!" Pastor Pipsner said. "It's time for bed. No playing in snow after baths, kids."

Hyacinth sighed. All through worship she listened to her dad but stared out the window, watching the big, fluffy flakes falling down to the ground. Snow! This was the day that kids looked forward to the minute all the leaves had fallen off the trees.

"Hyacinth?" her mother said.

Hyacinth pulled her attention away from the window.

"What?" Hyacinth asked.

"Your father asked you if you are thankful for anything today," her mother said.

"I'm thankful for snow!" Hyacinth said with a big grin.

"Nolan?" Pastor Pipsner said.

"I'm just praying the snow sticks to the ground and doesn't melt!" Nolan said.

"Good enough," said Pastor Pipsner. "Let's pray."

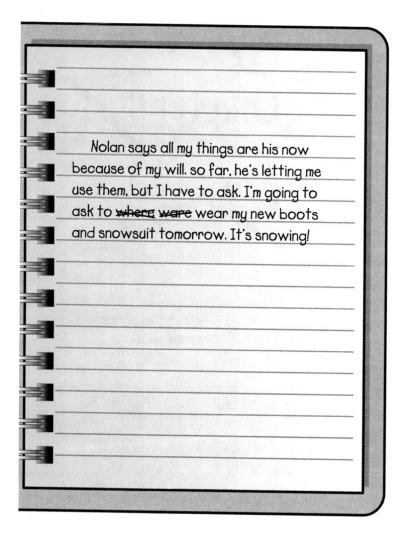

Nolan says all my things are his now because of my will. so far, he's letting me use them, but I have to ask. I'm going to ask to ~~where~~ ~~were~~ wear my new boots and snowsuit tomorrow. It's snowing!

Chapter 8

The next morning, as Pastor Pipsner was putting out their breakfast, Hyacinth danced around the kitchen in excitement.

"You'd better be careful," Pastor Pipsner said. "You're wearing slippery socks, and you might take a tumble."

"I won't!" Hyacinth said. "I'm just excited!"

"The snow will still be there after breakfast," her father said. "Sit down. It's your favorite—toaster waffles!"

Hyacinth planted herself down, but she couldn't help squirming in her seat.

"On second thought," her father said, "go call your brother to come eat."

"Nolan!" Hyacinth hollered.

"Not from here!" Pastor Pipsner said, wincing. "Go and get him without screaming across the house!"

But before Hyacinth could get up, Nolan appeared.

"Toaster waffles," Hyacinth said, by way of explanation.

"Let's say grace," Pastor Pipsner said. "Hyacinth, why don't you pray?"

"Dear God," Hyacinth prayed. "Thank You for the toaster waffles and for the syrup and for the orange juice. Amen."

"You didn't thank God for the forks," Nolan said.

"I don't have to!" Hyacinth said.

"Can you eat toaster waffles with no fork?" Nolan asked.

Hyacinth considered this for a moment, looking at the waffles and syrup. She was pretty sure that she could.

"Never mind, Nolan," their father said. "God wants us to thank Him without your interference. Eat up. The bus will be here soon."

As Hyacinth squeezed syrup on top of her toaster waffles, which were still hot from the toaster, Mrs. Pipsner came downstairs carrying her high-heeled shoes in one hand.

"Did you see the snow?" she asked Pastor Pipsner. "We'll have to brush the snow off the windows."

"Can I do it?" Hyacinth asked excitedly.

"No, Hyacinth," Pastor Pipsner said. "You have a bus to catch. Eat up."

"But you'd better both wear your snowsuits," their mother said. "I don't want you to be cold!"

"Oh, man!" Nolan said. "But there is only a little bit of snow!"

"Don't argue, Nolan," Mrs. Pipsner said. "Boots and snowsuits. And that's final!"

Hyacinth grinned so happily that she had trouble keeping her mouth closed as she chewed her toaster waffles. She had been waiting for this day for weeks and weeks, ever since they had bought the pretty pink moon boots and her snowsuit to match.

As soon as she had popped the last bite of waffle into her mouth, Hyacinth jumped up from the table and ran to find her snowsuit. She rummaged through the closet to find her scarf, mittens, and hat with a pom-pom on top.

"You still have a few minutes!" her mother called.

"I'll wait outside in the snow!" Hyacinth announced. She started to bundle herself up. Suddenly, a thought occurred to her, and she froze in her tracks.

"Nolan?" Hyacinth called. "Can I wear the pink moon boots?"

"OK," he called back.

With a nod, Hyacinth continued dressing until she was

bundled from head to toe. She had started to sweat a little. She waddled to the front door and tried to turn the handle. It was slippery in her mitten. She took off her mitten, opened the door, and waddled out into the crisp, cool air.

She could still see the grass poking out the top of the snow, but that didn't stop Hyacinth from stamping through it. Next, she got down on her hands and knees to taste it with the tip of her tongue. Then she tried making a snow angel. But it didn't look like much. All the snow was scraped away in the shape of her bundled arms and legs.

"What's wrong, Nolan?" Hyacinth asked, when her brother came out the front door with a scowl on his face.

"We look ridiculous!" he answered.

"Look!" she said. "I made a snowman!" The snowman was as tall as a pencil, and it took all the snow scraped up from as far as she could reach. She liked this snowman. He was very nice.

Nolan muttered something and stared down the street, watching for the bus. He pulled his hat off, just as their mother was coming out to go to the car to drive to work.

"Nolan, put your hat on!" she called. "It's cold out here!"

Nolan muttered something else and pulled his knitted hat back down over his ears.

"Do you realize that you look silly?" he said to his sister.

"I don't! I look great!" Hyacinth replied.

"You used up all the snow in the yard for your silly little snowman, and we're bundled up like we're at the North Pole!" he said.

Hyacinth looked down at herself. "I get to wear moon boots," she said.

"Me too," Nolan said miserably.

The sun was shining brightly, and Hyacinth could feel her head start to feel toasty hot on the top. She pulled off her mittens and tucked them in her pockets. Nolan stood unhappily in a circle of melted snow. Just then, the bus appeared at the end of the street.

"Wow, Nolan," Hyacinth said. "I'm glad that the snow stayed long enough for Mom to make us wear our snowsuits!"

"Oh, boy," Nolan sighed. And the bus doors opened.

Chapter 9

Nolan found out that the grade threes on the bus did not think it was exciting to wear a snowsuit without a big pile of snow. In fact, they thought it was funny! The younger kids, however, thought that Hyacinth's new pink moon boots were just as fantastic as Hyacinth thought they were.

In their classroom, all of the grade ones and twos wriggled out of their snowsuits, mittens, hats, scarves, and extra sweaters. Mrs. Raju announced that they were going to do something special.

"Today is our last day before Christmas break," Mrs. Raju

said. "We are going to make some Christmas tree decorations for your Christmas trees at home!"

"Oh, boy!" said Hyacinth. "I love crafting!"

Mrs. Raju passed out construction paper with shapes printed on it, glitter, glue, and baskets of markers that smelled like candy, fruit, and cinnamon. She passed out cotton balls to be used as snow, and each student got one candy cane wrapped in cellophane.

"Now it really feels like Christmas is coming!" Hyacinth whispered to Ruby.

"Uh-huh!" Ruby agreed, a marker lid in her mouth. She took it out. "Especially with the snow this morning!"

Hyacinth looked thoughtfully at the paper with the shapes drawn on it. She took out her scissors and carefully cut around the shapes' edges. She accidentally cut a few tips off the star, and she nearly cut the halo off the angel, but she stopped herself just in time, so the halo kind of hung down to the side. All in all, it wasn't a bad job!

"While you work, kids," Mrs. Raju said, "I am going to read the Christmas story to you and then we are going to talk about the meaning of Christmas!" Mrs. Raju opened a book. Hyacinth liked the way Mrs. Raju's black, shining hair hung down and swung like a curtain. Hyacinth thought that the angel over Bethlehem must have looked like Mrs. Raju.

·· Hyacinth Doesn't Miss Christmas ··

As Mrs. Raju read, Hyacinth opened her glue stick and twisted the bottom. She twisted it all the way up—until the whole stick of glue stuck out of the plastic container. Then she touched the side of the glue stick and rubbed her fingers on it. And then she twisted it back down. Now everything she touched stuck to her fingers, including the cotton ball. She pulled the cotton ball off her fingers with her teeth and carefully spit it into her lap.

"I like the part with the wise men the most," Ruby whispered.

"I like the donkey," Hyacinth said, "and the shepherds. They are good too!"

As Mrs. Raju kept reading, Hyacinth stuck cotton ball snow all over her star. Hyacinth thought she had never seen anything so elegant in her whole life. She held it up to look closer.

"Why is there snow on your star?" Lisa whispered.

"Because it's the Christmas star, of course!" Hyacinth said.

"There is no snow on stars," Lisa said.

"Maybe it is Santa fur," said Ruby.

"There is no Santa fur on stars, either," said Lisa primly.

Hyacinth raised her hand, and when Mrs. Raju didn't see her, she bounced up and down in her seat and flapped her hand like a fan.

"Yes, Hyacinth?" Mrs. Raju said.

"Is there such a thing as Santa fur?" asked Hyacinth. "Because I think there is and Lisa says there isn't."

"I said it isn't on stars!" said Lisa.

"Is there such a person as Santa Claus?" asked Mrs. Raju.

"He's your dad," said Claude.

"No, he's not; he's nobody!" said Nathan. "He's made up!"

"He's not as good as Baby Jesus," Hyacinth said.

"Why not?" asked Mrs. Raju.

"Because Jesus still loves you when you're bad," Hyacinth said.

"And if you're bad, Santa gives you coal for a present instead of video games," said Ruby.

"Let's finish the story," Mrs. Raju said, and began to read again.

"Hmm," Hyacinth said quietly, and she frowned.

"What?" Ruby asked in a whisper.

"Well, I have gotten into a lot of trouble this year," Hyacinth said.

"So?" said Ruby.

"Well, what if I get coal for Christmas?" asked Hyacinth.

"Santa isn't real," said Ruby.

"I know," said Hyacinth. "But presents are real, and I might get coal!"

"You *have* been kind of bad," Ruby agreed sadly.

"Oh, dear," Hyacinth sighed. "I wish I'd thought of this earlier!"

As Hyacinth worked on her star—the fluffy, cotton ball star with snow on it—she began to worry even more. Would her Christmas presents belong to Nolan too? Was there a rule somewhere that said that bad kids had to get coal? Was it a law, maybe, and her parents would have no choice?

"Recess time!" Mrs. Raju said. "Leave your crafts where they are, and we will continue with them when you come back in."

Everyone jumped up, including Ruby, but Hyacinth sat where she was.

"Don't worry," said Ruby. "Jesus loves us when we're bad too. We just need to say we're sorry and ask Him to help us be good next time."

"But it's my mom and dad who buy the presents!" Hyacinth sighed.

"True," Ruby said. "I hadn't thought of that."

Chapter 10

Hyacinth thought that recess was the best time of the day. It was fifteen whole minutes of playing outside, and she looked forward to recess more than anything else at school. But now, instead of playing outside, she was remembering that snowsuits can be very complicated. Sometimes, you can jump into them in no time at all, and other times, putting them on seems to take forever!

"What's taking so long?" Ruby asked.

"It's just—hard," Hyacinth wheezed, laying on her back to stick her legs into her snow pants. "As soon as I get my legs in, my pants get all pushed up inside my snow pants—I can't leave it like that!"

"But it's taking so long," Ruby sighed.

"Why don't you go save me a swing?" Hyacinth said.

"OK," said Ruby. "But hurry up, will you? Recess will be over!"

As Ruby dashed off to get a swing, Hyacinth stuck her arms down her snow pant leg to try and rearrange her pants inside. There was nothing more annoying than having your pants pushed up your legs inside your snow pants! But as soon as she got everything arranged and she stood up, Hyacinth realized she had her snow pants on backwards!

"Oh, for crying out loud!" Hyacinth said. That was what she heard her mother say when she was annoyed, and she liked the sound of it. But Hyacinth felt more than annoyed. This was turning out to be a hard day.

Hyacinth stamped out of her snow pants, Hyacinth kicked them across the hallway. She didn't need to wear her snow pants. She *wanted* to wear them. And they just wouldn't work!

"What are you doing?"

Hyacinth looked up to see Nolan watching her.

"What are *you* doing?" she retorted. "You're supposed to be in class!"

145

"I'm going to the bathroom," he said.

She looked at him doubtfully.

"Well, not right now, but I will in a minute," he said. "What are *you* doing?"

"Going out for recess," she said.

"You don't need to wear snow pants, you know," he said. "It's not cold outside."

At that, Hyacinth could feel her eyes welling up with tears. "I want to wear them!" she said. "I want to! I love my snow pants, and I just can't make them work!"

"I can help you," Nolan said.

"No!" said Hyacinth. "I don't want help! I want to do it myself!"

Nolan frowned and shrugged his shoulders. Hyacinth stamped back over to her snow pants and picked them up.

"Recess is almost over," she said mournfully. "And I'm going to get coal for Christmas."

"Coal?" said Nolan. "How come?"

"Because I have gotten into lots of trouble lately!" Hyacinth said. "I'm pretty sure there is a rule that says I have to get coal!"

"Nope," said Nolan.

"How do you know?" Hyacinth asked.

"Because Mom and Dad already bought your Christmas present, and I saw it," Nolan replied.

"You saw it?" Hyacinth gasped. "How? Did they show you?"

"No, I was looking for my present!" he said.

"Did you find it?" she asked.

"Yes," he replied. "I like it very much."

"That's bad, Nolan," Hyacinth said. "You deserve coal."

"But instead of coal, I'm getting some books and a sweater," he replied. "The sweater fits nicely."

"Nolan!" Hyacinth said. "It's really bad to try on your Christmas present before Christmas!"

"Do you want to know what you're getting?" Nolan asked with a grin.

"It doesn't matter," Hyacinth sighed. "Since I willed my things to you, I'm pretty sure that my Christmas presents will belong to you too."

"That's true," Nolan said with a thoughtful nod.

Hyacinth sighed. "This is a rough day," she said.

"I'll tell you what," said Nolan.

"What?" said Hyacinth.

"I can't change the law, and you did write up a legal document and all," Nolan said. "So while legally, all your things will belong to me, I will give them back to you!"

"You will?" Hyacinth asked, holding her breath.

"Yes," said Nolan. "I will give all your things back."

"Christmas presents too?" asked Hyacinth.

"Yes, I suppose so," he said.

"Oh, Nolan!" Hyacinth said, and she threw her arms around him.

"Stop it!" Nolan protested. "Quit it! Cut it out!"

"Nolan?"

Nolan and Hyacinth turned to see Nolan's teacher, Mr. Nelson, standing behind them with a curious look on his face.

"I thought you were on your way to the bathroom, Nolan," Mr. Nelson said.

"I was," said Nolan. "But my sister was crying."

"I was," Hyacinth admitted.

"Are you better now, Hyacinth?" Mr. Nelson asked.

"Yes, sir!" said Hyacinth. "The law is tricky business, but I think it's all right now!"

"All right, let's get going, Nolan," Mr. Nelson said.

"Hey, Nolan!" Hyacinth said.

"Yeah?" said Nolan.

"What *am* I getting for Christmas?" she asked.

"Coal," said Nolan. "But it will be your very own."

Hyacinth wasn't sure if he was joking or not, but she didn't have time to ask because the whistle blew and recess was over.

Chapter 11

Hyacinth loved making crafts. It was the best part of school, besides recess. She loved to write her name, *Hyacinth Gail Pipsner,* on the bottom of every creation she made. And next to her name, she would write her age, six and three-quarters.

"What are you making?" Ruby asked.

"Not another star," said Hyacinth. "But I want to use glitter, cotton balls, and loops of paper."

"Wow," said Ruby. "It sounds beautiful!"

"It will be," Hyacinth assured her. "I want my dad to put it on top of the tree."

Hyacinth bent over her new ornament, imagining all the wonderful things she would put on it. It would be spectacular—the best Christmas ornament ever! When she brought it home, her family would be speechless, staring in wonder at something so lovely. Her father would insist that they must put up their Christmas tree that very night so that the wonderful ornament could adorn the top of it. Her mother would look at it and wipe a little tear from her eye at the sheer beauty of that ornament.

Hyacinth took out her scissors and began to cut little strips of paper. Then she laid them out, ready for glitter.

"Please pass the glue," said Hyacinth.

Ruby passed the glue stick, and Hyacinth twisted the glue stick all the way up again. She looked at the glue stick. She sniffed it. It smelled a little bit sweet.

"It looks like a popsicle," said Hyacinth.

"It looks like the creamy kind," said Ruby.

"It smells kind of sweet," said Hyacinth.

"Does it taste sweet?" asked Ruby.

"Taste it!" said Hyacinth, holding it out in Ruby's direction.

"If I got caught tasting glue, my mother will put spinach in my lunch for a month," said Ruby. "I can't take the chance."

"*Hmm,*" said Hyacinth, and she began to put glue on her

strips of paper. Once they were all covered in glue, she began to sprinkle glitter on them.

"Better close the glue up, so it doesn't dry out," said Ruby.

So Hyacinth turned the dial on the bottom of the glue stick, and the stick of glue slowly moved back down into the plastic tube. As it moved down, a big glob of glue scraped off and fell onto Hyacinth's desk. Hyacinth looked at the glob of glue. She touched it with her finger. She picked it up and sniffed it. It still smelled sweet.

And Hyacinth popped it into her mouth.

Ruby stared at her in horror. "What have you done?" whispered Ruby. "And how does it taste?"

"Not great," Hyacinth said. "It tastes like glue."

"Do you want more?" asked Ruby, holding out the glue stick.

"No thanks," said Hyacinth. "That was enough."

"Does it taste like a popsicle?" asked Ruby. "The creamy kind?"

"Nope," said Hyacinth. "It tastes like sticky glue. I wonder if it will glue my teeth shut."

"My mother would kill me," Ruby whispered. "She really would!"

Hyacinth turned back to her craft. She tried to pay attention to the beautiful loops of glittery paper, but she kept thinking

about her mother. Her mother wouldn't be pleased, either, to know that she was eating glue. And she had told Hyacinth that if she ever ate something that was not food, she was supposed to tell a grown-up right away.

"I wonder if glue is bad for you," Hyacinth said.

"I wonder if it's poison!" Ruby said.

"It might be," Hyacinth agreed. "You never know."

"Like the weeds," said Ruby.

"And nail polish," said Hyacinth.

"You ate the nail polish?" Ruby asked, surprised.

"Don't ask," Hyacinth said, "it's a long story, and I don't look good in the end."

"OK," said Ruby.

Hyacinth tried to focus on her craft again, but she just couldn't put her heart into gluing down loops of glittery paper when she was wondering if the glue in her stomach was going to do something bad to her. She had escaped death by nail polish poisoning once. After that, it would be terrible to then be poisoned by a glue stick!

"Oh, no," Hyacinth sighed.

"What?" Ruby asked. "Do you feel sick?"

"No, but my mother told me if I ever eat anything again that isn't food, I have to tell a grown-up right away," she said.

"Mrs. Raju is the only grown-up here," said Ruby.

"I know," Hyacinth said sadly. "And I hate for Mrs. Raju to see me like this!"

Hyacinth looked at her unfinished craft for a long time, and then she slowly raised her hand into the air.

"Yes, Hyacinth?" said Mrs. Raju.

Hyacinth was silent.

"Hyacinth?" Mrs. Raju repeated.

Hyacinth took a deep breath and hung her head in shame. "Mrs. Raju," she said. "I ate glue."

The class, which had been abuzz with chatter and busy crafting, suddenly fell silent.

"You did?" said Mrs. Raju.

"Yes," Hyacinth said, her face burning with embarrassment.

Mrs. Raju came over to Hyacinth's desk and knelt down next to her. "Why?" she asked.

"To see what it tasted like," said Hyacinth.

"How much?" asked Mrs. Raju.

Hyacinth showed her with her fingers.

"All right," said Mrs. Raju. She stood up and went to the front of the room.

"Is she going to let you die as an example?" Ruby asked.

"I hope not!" Hyacinth whispered.

"Class!" Mrs. Raju said. "We have a new rule! There will be no eating of craft supplies!"

"Which ones?" Nathan asked.

"Any of them!" said Mrs. Raju firmly. "There will be no eating of paper, glitter, stickers, or glue. For any reason! No eating glue!"

"Does it taste good?" Lisa asked.

"How did it taste, Hyacinth?" Mrs. Raju asked.

"Bad," said Hyacinth.

"There you have it," Mrs. Raju said. "Glue tastes bad. Do not eat it. Do you all understand?"

The class nodded and murmured their agreement.

"Good!" said Mrs. Raju, and she went back to her desk.

Hyacinth raised her hand again.

"Mrs. Raju?" Hyacinth said.

"Yes, Hyacinth."

"Will I die?" asked Hyacinth.

"Not today," Mrs. Raju said. "But I will have to send a letter home to your parents."

"Oh, dear," sighed Hyacinth. "I might die yet."

Chapter 12

That night, when Hyacinth got home from school, the Christmas tree was set up and ready to be decorated.

"You put up the tree!" Hyacinth hollered. "This is great!"

"There is something even better," her father said. "Look who is here for the holidays!"

And there, standing in the kitchen, wearing slacks and a soft, silky blouse, was Hyacinth's grandma!

"Grandma!" Hyacinth squealed.

"Grandma!" Nolan yelled.

And they ran to give their grandmother big hugs.

That evening, even though the snow had melted away, Hyacinth felt like Christmas had truly arrived. The tree was set up, and they got to hang the ornaments.

"I'm a little worried, Grandma," Hyacinth said.

"Why?" asked Grandma.

"Well, you might have heard, but I have been getting into lots of trouble lately," Hyacinth said.

"For what?" asked Grandma.

"Eating things," said Hyacinth.

"Yes, I'd heard," Grandma said.

"Have you also heard about kids getting coal for Christmas if they are bad?" asked Hyacinth.

"I've heard of it," Grandma said.

"Well, I'm thinking I might get some coal this year," Hyacinth sighed. "And that worries me!"

"Oh, I wouldn't worry about that!" Grandma chuckled.

"It's hard not to!" said Hyacinth seriously. "The law being what it is, these days."

Grandma gave Hyacinth a funny look.

"Nolan?" Grandma called. "What have you been telling your sister?"

"Nothing!" he said.

"Are you sure?" she asked.

"It's hard to remember everything I say," Nolan said. "I say so many things—"

·· **Hyacinth Doesn't Miss Christmas** ··

Grandma shook her head and laughed. "Hyacinth, one day you are going to get really mad at that brother of yours," she said, "and I want you to remember that you only have one brother!"

"OK," said Hyacinth with a shrug. "He was very nice to me today, though, Grandma. And I think I want to make him a special Christmas present!"

"Really?" said Grandma. "What would you like to make him?"

"Something with loops of paper and cotton balls and glitter," said Hyacinth. "I'm quite good at those!"

So that evening, Grandma and Hyacinth sat down at the table with craft supplies. Hyacinth colored some paper strips very carefully with markers, pressing so hard that the markers squeaked across the paper. When she was done, she picked up the glue stick and opened the lid.

"I could use a snack," Hyacinth said. "I'm kind of hungry." She sat looking down into the tube thoughtfully.

"Hyacinth," Grandma said.

"Yes?" said Hyacinth.

"Don't eat that," said Grandma.

Hyacinth looked up with an impish grin.

"It doesn't taste good anyway," Hyacinth said with a shrug. "I was thinking more along the lines of cookies."

"Cookies I can do!" said Grandma.

That night before she went to bed, Hyacinth pulled out her journal. She wanted to write a prayer about being alive.

dear God,

I didn't die, and that's really good! I'm happy to be alive, and I'll tell You why.

Nolan would get all the good stuff if I was dead, and that wouldn't be fair.

I like to eat. I really like to eat spakheti. Not only does it taste good but it's funn to wrap around the fork.

I think I'd miss my mom and dad a lot. well, maybe; I would be ~~ded~~ dead so I wouldn't know it but I know it now and I think I'd miss my mom and dad a lot.

I'd miss my grandma. She makes the best Christmas cookies!

I'd miss Christmas. That would be terrible!

I think You'd miss me. because You and I are special friends. right??? so I think You'd miss me. I'm just saying.

So I'll talk to You again later. but for now. I'm going to ask my dad to give me a cookie before bed. Please. please. please let him give me a cookie!

most sincerely.
Hyacinth Gail Pipsner

READY TO RIDE

Are You Ready To Ride?

Read all about three BFFs—Kendra, Ruth-Ann, and Megan—the horses they love, and the important character-building lessons they learn as they form the Ready to Ride riding club. You'll love this awesome series for girls just like you!

Series books one to three available as a set only

A Perfect Star, Zippitty Do Dah, and **Good As Gold, Books 1–3, #4333003844**

Series Book Four   **Series Book Five**   **Series Book Six**

Blondie's Big Ride
#0816322252

A Friend for Zipper
#0816322260

Super Star Problems
#0816322554

READY TO RIDE SERIES